"I thought we were going to crash!"

"That, Miss Hannelly, was the point." A.J.'s voice lashed like a whip. "Because you're an accident waiting for a place to happen. Just be glad I didn't send the plane into a screaming dive—or any of the other tactics we use with bad-risk students." He reached to open his door. "And if you don't like my lessons, Miss Hannelly, you'd better quit right now."

He exited the aircraft, leaving Lissa to stay or follow as she pleased.

"You'd just love that, wouldn't you?" she yelled at him from the doorway. "Well, you're not getting rid of me that easily! No matter how many times you make a fool of me, I'm not giving up!"

A.J. gave her a long, hard look. "Well, well, what a surprise. I thought little Miss Happy-go-lucky would be sobbing on my shoulder by now." But despite his sarcasm, there was an almost begrudging hint of admiration in his voice.

Anne Marie Duquette has traveled extensively throughout the United States, first as an air force "brat" and then as a member of the military herself. She started her writing career as a young girl, with lengthy letters to relatives and friends describing her impressions of countless new duty locations. Now married to a naval petty officer and the mother of two young children, she continues to travel, but considers the Rocky Mountains her real "home."

Arrangement with a Rebel is her fourth Harlequin Romance novel, and the third one set in Colorado.

Books by Anne Marie Duquette

HARLEQUIN ROMANCE
2918—AN UNLIKELY COMBINATION
3080—UNLIKELY PLACES
3151—ADVENTURE OF THE HEART

Don't miss any of our special offers. Write to us at the following address for information on our newest releases.

Harlequin Reader Service
P.O. Box 1397, Buffalo, NY 14240
Canadian address: P.O. Box 603,
Fort Erie, Ont. L2A 5X3

ARRANGEMENT WITH A REBEL

Anne Marie Duquette

Harlequin Books

TORONTO • NEW YORK • LONDON
AMSTERDAM • PARIS • SYDNEY • HAMBURG
STOCKHOLM • ATHENS • TOKYO • MILAN
MADRID • WARSAW • BUDAPEST • AUCKLAND

With much gratitude to
Former Instructor Pilot
Lt. Colonel James S. Villotti
United States Air Force (Retired)
for his technical assistance.
Thanks, Dad!

ISBN 0-373-03212-9

Harlequin Romance first edition August 1992

ARRANGEMENT WITH A REBEL

CHAPTER ONE

"I'M SORRY, Miss Hannelly, but there's absolutely no way I can pass you. No way at all."

Lissa Hannelly stared at her flight examiner with dismay. "But I've put in all the required hours! I've passed all my written tests! You *have* to certify me as a pilot!"

The examiner shook his head regretfully. "You're a terrible pilot. It's no surprise you failed your final flight test. I'm sorry, Miss Hannelly—but you're the worst student I've seen in twenty years of teaching!" He paused, shrugging. "Perhaps someone else could help you?"

Lissa heard the dismissal in his voice and gave a frustrated sigh. "I've tried other people. You're the fourth examiner I've engaged," she admitted.

The examiner's eyes widened in obvious surprise. "Perhaps you should consider giving up the idea of getting a pilot's license," he advised. "You know air time's expensive, and if *four* qualified examiners won't pass you..." His voice trailed off.

Lissa fumed at his tacit assessment of her ability. True, she hadn't passed her final flight exam yet, but that didn't mean she *couldn't*.

"I'll get my license. I'm not giving up until I do!"

The examiner gazed openly at Lissa, taking in the blue-gray eyes narrowed with determination, and the stubborn jut of her chin. "Well, you aren't a quitter, anyway," he said, rubbing his own chin thoughtfully. "You know, there might be someone who can help you..."

Lissa eagerly pounced on his words. "Who?"

"His name is A.J. Corbett. He was a top instructor in the military until he was pensioned out with ruptured eardrums."

"Ruptured eardrums?" Lissa bit her lip, praying the man was still healthy enough to take her on as a student. The law said she had to successfully complete a flight course with an instructor, then go before a Federal Aviation Administration flight examiner for the final air test. She'd passed the flight course—just barely—but so far, she hadn't passed the certifying exam.

"That's right. A.J. was flying a rescue mission, and he lost his cabin pressure in the attempt. Once you rupture an eardrum, the military won't let you fly jets anymore. They offer you a desk job or let you out with a medical discharge." The instructor shook his head. "A desk job wasn't for A.J., so now he flies his own planes. Not only is he the best instructor I know, he's a certified FAA flight examiner. You know your instructor can't also be your examiner, but since you've already put in your hours, he could help you pass the test—if he took you on."

"You know him? You really think he can help me?" Lissa asked hopefully. She opened her purse and rummaged for a pen and some paper. "Do you have his address and phone number?"

"Yes, but..." The examiner hesitated. "There's a slight problem. A.J. doesn't instruct on a regular basis."

Lissa felt her rising hopes suddenly falter. "What do you mean?"

The man shrugged. "A.J. likes life in the fast lane. You know, fast cars, fast planes, fast—"

He broke off, and Lissa wondered if he had been about to say "fast women."

"He's a pylon racer. A.J. only gives flight lessons during the off season, and that won't be for months."

"Great." Lissa rolled her eyes in dismay. Pylon racers flew circular laps around huge pylons, much as formula cars raced around circular speed tracks. She'd always thought the sport dangerous, foolhardy and a shameful waste of fuel. Couldn't a skilled pilot like this A.J. Corbett think of better ways to spend his time?

"Just what I need, a crazy pylon racer."

"A.J.'s pretty good at it," the examiner said, his voice admiring. "In fact, he's good at anything that has to do with planes. And he's a great trainer. His success with hopeless students is legendary, both in the military and out. If anyone can get you in shape to pass the final flight exam, he can."

Lissa ignored the implied insult and waited, her pen poised.

"I don't know if you'll be able to hire him, though. He's preparing for another race," the examiner warned. "The September Reno National, I think."

"I'll take my chances," Lissa insisted. "Where can I find him?"

The man looked out the nearest window of his office and pointed up. "See that Cessna getting ready to touch down?"

She thrust pen and paper back into her purse and hurried over to the window with its view of the Colorado Rocky Mountains in the distance, and the runways of Jefferson County Airport, more commonly known as JeffCo, in the foreground. JeffCo was at the base of the Hogback Range. Lissa let her eyes rest on the familiar shape of the land, then drift north toward Golden, the closest big town and the Jefferson County seat. It was from there that the Cessna was approaching.

"You mean that 152 Aerobat?" she asked, not concealing her envy or her admiration. The Aerobat was an acrobatic plane specially built and approved for spins, rolls, loops and other risky flying maneuvers. Although she disapproved of activities like pylon racing, she was well aware of the high level of skill required to do that kind of flying. Intrigued, Lissa found herself looking forward to meeting the plane's owner.

"That's the one. A.J.'s the pilot. If I could make a suggestion?" he said as Lissa got ready to leave.

"Yes?"

"I know you really want to learn to fly, but let me warn you, if A.J. says no, he means no. Once he makes up his mind, that's it." The examiner studied Lissa in a way that made her uncomfortably conscious of her short, curvy figure and her cap of unruly light brown curls. "That goes for pretty women, too. You know what A.J.'s code name was in the military?"

Lissa shook her head.

"*Rebel,* and it fits him. He isn't about to take orders from anyone, especially a washout student. He makes his own rules."

"I don't care what rules he makes. I'm desperate."

"For your sake, I hope you can come to some kind of terms."

"I'll agree to any arrangement, even one with a rebel," Lissa declared. Seeing that the plane had landed, she moved toward the door. "Thanks for the help."

"Good luck. You're going to need it," the examiner warned.

Lissa fleetingly wondered if he meant that she needed luck getting her license or luck engaging A.J. as her examiner, but she didn't stop to ask. She was already outside in the July air. The temperature had risen to the mid-seventies, a welcome warmth all too rare in these high altitudes, but Lissa didn't stop to bask in the sun. She had more important things on her mind. Her grandparents owned Hannelly Air Charter, a small two-plane operation that would go out of business without another pilot. She was to be that pilot—if she could ever get her license.

The Cessna had slowed its taxi to park in its appointed space so Lissa quickened her steps. She reached the plane just as the gleaming metal door opened and the pilot climbed out. Long, jean-clad muscular legs were followed by a tall, trim body. She saw the pilot's strong-featured face in profile as he locked the door behind him.

Lissa felt a jolt of pure feminine awareness. This man was bursting with vitality. The sun glinted on sun-streaked brown hair as he jumped easily to the pavement. A steady hand lifted the sunglasses from his eyes, their piercing, sky-colored depths catching her gaze.

"Can I help you?"

Lissa noticed the quick assessing look that preceded his smile. She knew instinctively that this man didn't miss much.

Lissa glanced at the plane again, making sure it was the same Cessna Aerobat she'd observed landing. "Are you Mr. Corbett?"

"If you're looking for Andrew James Corbett, you have the right man. What can I do for you?"

Lissa glanced at the clipboard tucked underneath his arm. "If you aren't busy, Mr. Corbett—"

"Call me A.J. And you're ... ?"

"Lissa." She didn't give her last name, afraid that her reputation as a student would end the conversation before it even began. "I'd like to talk with you for a few minutes."

A.J. nodded. "Well, Lissa, I'm all through for the day, but I was headed to the Flight Line for something to eat." He checked his watch. "Have you had lunch? We can talk over some food. I'm starved."

Lissa didn't get a chance to reply. He pressed his palm against the small of her back, guiding her toward the row of buildings along the runway that made up the Flight Line, which included the cafeteria. Lissa turned in surprise at his touch, but they were already moving along, A.J. adjusting his strides to match hers.

He *did* make his own rules, Lissa thought wryly. Runway traffic and noise had increased, and it wasn't until they were inside that they were able to talk. Ten minutes later they were seated with hamburgers, French fries and cups of coffee.

"What can I do for you, Lissa?" A.J. asked with unmistakable interest.

"I'd like you to teach me to fly."

A.J.'s interest immediately died, much to her dismay. He took a bite of his hamburger and a swallow of coffee before answering. "I'm sorry. It's racing season. I don't have time to instruct student pilots right now."

Lissa was prepared for that. "The Reno National air races aren't until September. It's only July."

One of his eyebrows lifted ever so slightly. "Late July, but that's beside the point. I need to practice and prepare my planes."

"I know, but I wouldn't take much of your time." Lissa ignored her own food as she watched A.J. concentrate on his. "All I need is to pass the final flight test with a flight examiner. My . . . previous examiner recommended you."

The attack on the hamburger was momentarily suspended. "You've already had lessons?"

"Yes. I've put in all the ground and air time for my private pilot's license."

"And you weren't able to get it?"

Lissa mentally squirmed, but there was no way around the truth. "No. I've had four different examiners," she said baldly. "And four flight instructors. I still couldn't get certified."

A.J. put the half-finished hamburger back on his plate and gave Lissa his full attention. "May I have their names, please?"

Lissa recited them. A.J. let out a slow whistle. "They don't get much better than that."

"I know," Lissa agreed ruefully. "But none of them was willing to certify me. I was told if anyone could help me get my license, you could."

A.J. picked up his hamburger again. "I'm sorry. I've told you, I don't teach during racing season."

"But I'll pay! I'll pay whatever you want, if you'll only take me on! I'm sure you can use the money. Pylon racing's expensive. You can't expect to win all the time."

A.J. finished the last bite of burger, then carelessly wiped his fingers with a paper napkin. "I don't race for the money, I race for the thrill. Don't get me wrong, I enjoy instructing, but my first love is pylon racing. I only teach during the off-season. It's as simple as that."

Lissa's heart sank, her disappointment visible.

"Why is it so important for you to learn to fly?" A.J. asked curiously. "After your repeated failures—" Lissa winced at his bluntness "—surely you can see the logic in quitting."

"You don't understand. My grandparents own a charter service. We have two planes, and we used to have two pilots."

"Used to?"

"Yes. My grandfather flies one plane, and his assistant flew the other."

"What happened?" A.J. eyed her untouched hamburger as he spoke, and Lissa pushed her plate toward him. "Here, take it. I'm not hungry."

"Are you sure?" he asked.

"Yes," she said irritably. A.J. seemed more interested in her food than her story, but she was determined to go on.

"Terry Martin, our assistant, was grounded. He was never one to watch his weight, and he developed high blood pressure. He lost his license when he couldn't pass the flight physical."

A.J. frowned, as if he had no respect for people who didn't take care of themselves. "So what's the problem? Why don't you just hire another pilot?"

She sighed. "We can't afford it. I can barely afford flying lessons as it is. Things are tight financially at the moment, because our older plane needs repairs. Terry didn't mind working for a low salary because—" Lissa hesitated "—well, just because."

Terry had hoped for certain fringe benefits from Lissa that she'd refused to bestow. He'd even proposed marriage. Lissa was fond of Terry, but somehow she hadn't quite been able to make that final commitment.

"I see." A.J.'s expression hardened, and she flushed.

"I don't think you do," she said angrily. "Terry wants to marry me. That's why he's still working for such a low salary. I turned him down, but he won't leave. He's loyal to our company. He's staying on to help out our mechanic. He's not there for . . . for . . ."

The coldness left A.J.'s face to be replaced by a slow, lazy smile. "Special favors? Well, seeing what a lovely lady you are, I can't say I blame him for trying." He gave her figure the full attention that previously only the hamburger had received.

Lissa didn't like the way she found herself enjoying his evident appreciation. So he did have appetites for other things besides food—but that had nothing to do with her. After his earlier disinterest, Lissa suspected that A.J. Corbett's sudden charm was simply meant to smooth her ruffled feathers. She felt slightly insulted, but had too much to lose to be distracted now.

"We were awarded a government bid that requires two planes, Mr. Corbett. Once I get my license, I'm willing to work for no salary until we get our other plane back in top condition. I've passed my ground-school test, and I've logged all the flight time required to get certified. But I haven't been able to pass the final flight exam. I just need someone who'll work with me a little before they give me the final.''

A.J. slowly shook his head. "I can appreciate your problem, Lissa, but as I told you, I can't spare the time to instruct during racing season."

"I'm a quick learner. It won't take you long to pass me." She studied the man before her, attracted by his easy self-assurance—and by something else she couldn't define. "Please, won't you reconsider?" she pleaded.

"I'm sorry."

Lissa's heart sank. She wouldn't get to work with A.J. now, was her first thought. She didn't have time to analyze that reaction, though, because A.J. was still talking.

"If it's really important to you, I can recommend some other examiners," he offered.

"Thanks, but that may be too late to save my grandfather's bid with the ranger station," Lissa said, bitterly disappointed. How could she explain to her grandparents that she'd failed as a pilot—again? She stared out the window at the air traffic, wondering what unlucky star prevented her from being part of it.

A.J. froze at her words. "Ranger station? Your last name wouldn't be Hannelly, would it?"

"Yes. Have you heard of us? Hannelly Air Charter provides the charter service for the ranger station up in Gunnison County."

"I know. Well, I'll be."

Lissa couldn't help but notice Andrew Corbett's sudden interest. She turned back to face him again. "Does that make a difference?"

A.J. said nothing. He busied himself stirring his coffee, but Lissa knew a delaying tactic when she saw one. He wasn't about to change his mind.

And she'd never learn to fly. Maybe her grandfather could try to get a loan from the bank to tide them over. The loan officers had rejected his application the first time, but perhaps if he tried again...

"I'll do it," A.J. said abruptly.

Lissa's head snapped up, her short brown curls bobbing. "You will?" she asked excitedly. And in the next breath, "Why?"

"Why what?" A.J. finished the last of his coffee.

"This change of heart. You refused to have anything to do with instructing me, and then this about-face. Why?"

"Let's just say I like a challenge," A.J. replied, his face suspiciously blank.

Lissa mentally reviewed the conversation. "You changed your mind right after I told you we serviced the remote ranger station," she said with certainty. "Why would that make you give up your racing time?"

"Smart lady." There was a glimmer of respect in his eyes. "If you must know, there's a woman up at the ranger station I see from time to time. Her name's Alanna, and lately I've neglected her shamefully. I don't have government clearance to land at the ranger station airstrip, so I can't get up there very often. With you and your charter clearance, I can see Alanna more often."

"Oh." So A.J. had a girlfriend. Well, it was to be expected. He was intelligent and attractive—if you liked devil-may-care men who raced around pylons and flew Aerobats. Lissa suddenly wondered how it would feel to sit beside him in a fast plane on a race course, then pushed the thought from her mind. Why should she care? She needed an examiner, she told herself, nothing else.

"Would you like any more specifics, or is the lady's name enough?" A.J. asked coolly.

"I'm not interested in your love life," was Lissa's tart—and untruthful—response. She should know better than to waste time speculating about what kind of woman would appeal to A.J. She had problems enough on her hands.

"Good. Now let's settle the terms of our... arrangement. I'll instruct you on two conditions."

"Anything!"

A.J. lifted one eyebrow, and Lissa willed herself not to redden. The worst thing was, she suspected his air of sensuality wasn't deliberate. It had nothing to do with fancy after-shaves or tight clothes; A.J. wore neither. But there was still that air about him.

"Well, almost anything," she qualified, annoyed that her blush appeared anyway. Even with Terry she'd never colored at suggestive remarks, and Terry was rarely subtle.

"One, you don't pay me. I instruct you free of charge."

Lissa blinked in surprise. Her grandfather certainly wouldn't mind that condition, but she had to ask, "Are you sure? I can pay."

A.J. waved his hand dismissively. "That's debatable, after what you've just told me. But I don't need your money. Just pitting my teaching abilities against such a challenge—and succeeding—is payment enough."

Lissa didn't know whether to be insulted or pleased. After a moment's hesitation, she said, "If you insist." No need to look a gift horse in the mouth. "And the second condition?"

A.J. gave her a steady look. "I've taught a lot of students in my day, and the bad ones all shared one characteristic—a poor attitude."

"Oh?" Lissa's voice held frosty disdain.

"A poor attitude," A.J. repeated emphatically. "You're young enough to have good reflexes, and I'm assuming you're intelligent enough to grasp the mechanics of flying. I'd bet my bottom dollar your failure to get certified is due to your attitude."

Lissa opened her mouth to speak, then thought better of it and reined in her temper. She had to be honest with herself. Lately she'd been worried about more than just the business. She'd been worried about her own skills and abilities; with each defeat, she lost further confidence. *Something* had to be wrong with her or she wouldn't keep failing like this.

"Go on," she said, her voice curt.

"Usually poor attitudes in pilots come from being unprepared. You don't expect the worst, so you aren't equipped to deal with emergencies. Poor pilots wear the proverbial rose-colored glasses. They expect everything to go just perfectly for them. But you can't let takeoffs become routine, even if you've performed hundreds of them successfully. You can't expect the weather always to stay sunny. In short, you have to anticipate the worst and be ready for it."

"I'm always careful," Lissa said a little defiantly. "What bothers me is your negative attitude to life. It seems out of place for an instructor."

"You're wrong. There's a difference between having a negative attitude and flying defensively. I'm smart enough to know the difference. Are you?"

He folded both arms on the table and leaned closer. Lissa found herself staring right into his eyes.

"I'll bet you're a terrible driver," he said with certainty. "I'll bet you've received speeding tickets because you weren't paying attention to the road signs. You've probably run a few lights because you were busy daydreaming. I'll even wager that you've been involved in a fender bender or two."

It was true; she *had* been involved in some minor traffic accidents. She always drove carefully, but things just seemed to spring up out of nowhere. By the time she figured out what was going on, it was usually too late.

Lissa's face had obviously betrayed her. "Aha!" A.J. pounced on her like a cat on a mouse. "I knew I was right. Lord help the rest of us in the sky when you're behind the controls."

Lissa started to reach for her purse, planning to leave, but stopped abruptly. She had nowhere else to turn. Where else could she find a flight examiner willing to work with her? Besides, she had the glimmerings of an intuition that A.J. might, just might, be correct.

A.J. watched the play of emotions across her face. "If I agree to take you on as a student, you have to agree to let me change your attitudes about flying."

Lissa sighed. "All right. I don't seem to be having much luck on my own."

"And you'll have to change your approach to life in general, the way I see it. Those rose-colored glasses have got to go."

"Now wait just a minute! I think you're carrying this a little far, Mr. Corbett. My personal life is no concern of yours."

"Wrong again, Miss Hannelly. When I take on a student, I own her, body and soul, for the duration of the course."

To her amazement, Lissa saw that he was serious. "You're too young to be telling other people how to live their lives!" she exclaimed.

"How old are you, Miss Hannelly?"

"I'm twenty-five," Lissa admitted.

"Twenty-five. I'm thirty-two now. At twenty-five I was already a qualified jet pilot. I was instructing hundreds of other men to become the same. I was also preparing for my next command as a squadron leader, which I was awarded two years later. Tell me, what have you accomplished in *your* aviation career? I'm not talking about all the free plane rides you've taken with your grandfather or your boyfriend."

His voice was deceptively soft, but Lissa felt its sting. That easy sensuality he wore was gone, replaced by a strength Lissa recognized—and envied.

"Well?"

She swallowed hard. A.J. had certainly put his point across. "Not much."

"I see. Under the circumstances, I'm prepared to state that I know more about flying than you do. And as I'll be risking my time, my plane and, more importantly, my life, sitting next to a woman who's gone through *four* examiners..." He raised one eyebrow expressively.

Lissa's cheeks burned with shame, and she had difficulty meeting his gaze.

"I really think you'd better accept my terms."

Lissa was trembling. She could back out now; she could back out and play it safe, the way she had all her life. A.J. was throwing her a professional challenge she didn't think she could handle. But with the situation at home, did she dare give up?

She lifted her chin and managed to keep her voice calm. "If changing my attitude is truly in my best interests—" she took a deep breath "—then yes, I agree. And Terry's not my boyfriend," she added quickly.

A.J. nodded, apparently satisfied.

"But first you'll have to convince me that it is," she insisted. "In my best interests, I mean."

"Oh, I will, Lissa. Have no doubts about that."

This man represented more than a professional challenge, Lissa realized. Whether he knew it or not, there was something about him that challenged her personally, too. This time, Lissa met his gaze without flinching. "You certainly like things your own way, don't you?"

"When it comes to staying alive in a plane, yes, I do." A.J.'s voice was deadly serious.

"You get me my license, and I'll dance to any tune you play," she replied just as serious as he. "I have a lot riding on this."

"Then be here tomorrow, ready to work. I'll see you at 10 a.m. And that's military time, not running-behind-schedule-charter-service time."

"I keep my appointments," Lissa said, annoyed. "You don't have to be sarcastic about it."

"Oh, I intend to do more than that. You'll either pass my flight exam with flying colors, or you'll wish you'd never left the ground."

"And what's that supposed to mean?"

"It means you're not the only one here with something at stake."

Lissa gave him a disdainful look. "Saving my family's livelihood hardly compares with extra trips out to see your girlfriend."

For a second A.J.'s eyes flashed cold. "There's more to it than that." At Lissa's startled expression, he abruptly broke off. "Goodbye, Lissa. Remember, ten sharp tomorrow."

"But..." Lissa watched him leave. She should be rejoicing in her good fortune; instead, she was uneasy. It wasn't what "Rebel" Corbett had said that worried her.

It was what he hadn't said.

CHAPTER TWO

"Isn't it great, Grandma? I get free instruction from a top pilot!"

Lissa was at the dinner table, telling everyone a cheerful, modified version of her meeting with A.J. Corbett. She praised only his professional virtues and kept the fact that she was personally intrigued by him to herself. She doubted if the men at the table would understand, especially Terry. No matter how innocent her sudden interest in A.J. might be, Terry had a jealous streak that Lissa preferred to avoid.

"If you'd passed four examiners ago, this wouldn't be necessary," her grandfather grumbled. "We could be using that money to get your instrument rating and commercial license." Will Hannelly speared another piece of meat loaf. "If you don't get at least your private license soon, I don't know how we'll manage to make all the runs the ranger station needs. Between ferrying their staff back and forth to Denver and bringing in supplies from Gunnison, I have my hands full. That doesn't include flying you in to JeffCo every time you find a new examiner, either."

Lissa stiffened with embarrassment. JeffCo was miles east of Hannelly Air Charter, too far to drive. Unfortunately she'd failed to get her private license with the two flight examiners in the area. Without it, she was ineligible to advance to any higher certification.

"She's trying, Will," Margaret Hannelly said softly, and Lissa threw her grandmother a look of gratitude.

"If Terry here would stay on his diet and take his medication like he's supposed to, maybe he'd get his blood pressure back down, and we wouldn't be in this mess," Will continued to complain.

Terry wisely decided to put back the ladle without the desired second helping of gravy and mashed potatoes. Will wasn't pleased that he hadn't passed his last two flight physicals.

"As it is, I don't understand how *you* can't manage to get your license." Will stabbed an accusing fork in Lissa's direction. "I had no problems. And your father certainly had no problems getting his license, either. Now, *there* was a pilot. Why can't you take after him?"

"Will, that's enough!" Margaret ordered. "If our son was such a good pilot, where is he today?"

Lissa's own fork clattered to her plate. She pushed her chair away and hurried from the table. Seven years ago, and the memory still hurt. Her father had left with a load of supplies one morning, her mother riding along to keep him company. A freak summer blizzard had sprung up in the mountains, radio contact had been lost, and that was that. Nathan and Rose Hannelly were gone. Condolences were offered, the insurance company had replaced the plane, and Lissa's young eyes took on a sorrow rarely seen in eighteen-year-old girls.

It was then that Lissa's grandfather had asked her to learn to fly, but Lissa flatly, almost hysterically, refused. The thought of replacing her father, taking over his job, was too distressing for her to even consider. Terry Martin had been hired instead. He was a local pilot, capable and easy to get along with. He was also the only man her own age that Lissa ever spent much time with, because her grandfather's business was far off the beaten track.

Hannelly Air Charter was situated halfway between the county seat of Gunnison and the remote ranger station. The company was awarded the service contract to the station precisely because of its location. Her grandfather had his own private runway, only a twenty-minute flight from the ranger station. His airstrip was also a short flight from Gunnison, too, where he had ready access to supplies for the station.

The family had always been close. Three generations of Hannellys, along with Leo, the old mechanic, had all lived on the premises. The Hannellys shared the large family house, while Leo and later Terry had quarters in the office building off the hangar.

When Lissa's parents disappeared, the family relationships begin to shift. Lissa was as close to her grandmother as ever, but with the death of his only child, her grandfather withdrew from everyone. The absence of her parents left a void in Lissa's life that Terry was only too willing to fill. Everyone, especially Terry, assumed that some day they would marry, no matter what Lissa said.

"You okay, Lissa?"

Lissa had let herself out of the house and found refuge on a bench under the trees. She didn't turn around at Terry's approach, but continued to stare at the surrounding mountains. The deciduous trees were in full summer leaf.

"It's so awful." Her voice was sad. "I wonder if I'll ever get used to them being gone."

Terry leaned against the rough boards of the pine rail fence that separated the huge front yard from the landing area. "Your parents? Probably not." Then, as he usually did with unpleasant subjects, Terry began to speak of something else. "Too bad your grandmother never learned to fly. Both of us would be off the hook. I hope this Corbett guy is as good as you say he is, and you get your license soon."

Lissa turned toward him at that, and found herself comparing Terry with A.J. Corbett. The two men were both attractive, although A.J. had a hard, razor-sharp edge to his looks that Terry Martin lacked. With his wide, heavily lashed eyes, plump cheeks and wavy hair, Terry looked like a cuddly teddy bear. No one could say that of A.J. Corbett. His eyes were too shrewd, the chin too strong and the chiseled nose too sharp to come close to resembling a stuffed animal.

There was a worldliness about Corbett that Lissa recognized and secretly envied. He wasn't really much older than her, but there was no comparison between them when it came to self-assurance. She sensed that he was a man who stood on his own two feet and only respected those who did the same. But she had no idea what motivated him, what drove him to compete, for instance. Someone like A.J. could take forever to get to know.

Terry wasn't like that. Lissa felt she knew him very well indeed. She wondered if that was because there weren't many facets to Terry's personality, then guiltily rejected that traitorous thought. Still, she couldn't help remembering how A.J. had immediately singled out her attitude problem. No one else, including Terry, had been able to suggest why she couldn't pass her flight exam. She hadn't even been able to identify the reason herself, although she knew there had to be one.

"Your grandfather talked to Leo, and Leo's agreed to fly you back and forth to JeffCo for your lessons," Terry announced.

"Leo? He hates to fly! That's why he became a mechanic. I'm surprised his license is still valid."

Terry nodded. "So was I. But with your grandfather working shorthanded, he can't afford the time to fly you. Leo's volunteered. Will even tried to get him to help with the trips out to the ranger station, but he stated flat out he'd only fly you, not supplies."

Lissa smiled. "Leo's a sweetheart."

"He does have a soft spot for you," Terry said. He joined her on the bench. "Just like I do," he said as he reached for her arm to pull her close.

"Terry, don't." Lissa squirmed as he tried to kiss her.

"Why not? You know I want to marry you."

Lissa pushed him away. "We're not engaged, Terry."

Terry sighed. "I refuse to give up. Why won't you let me buy you a ring?"

Lissa stood up and went to lean against the fence. "I care about you, Terry, but I'm not in love with you. Even if I was, you can't afford to get married. You don't even get a salary anymore. What are you going to do if you can't pass your physical and get your license back?"

"I'll get it," Terry said confidently.

"But what if you don't? How would we live? I'm only an odd-jobs worker at a small charter service. I couldn't get a decent-paying job, either. Terry, I'm worried about the business," she said suddenly.

"What are you talking about?"

"I..." Lissa hesitated, afraid to voice what she'd hidden so long. "I'm worried about Grandfather. He's getting old. He hasn't been the same since my parents disappeared, and I wonder if he should retire."

"How can you say that? Will's as sharp as a tack. If he heard you talking like this he'd have your hide."

"I know, but he needs a rest. So does that older plane..." Lissa nervously twisted her watch on her wrist. "I'm worried about it, too. We bought it at the same time we got the one my parents crashed in. That was years ago. We can't afford to replace it, and Grandfather's too old to be doing the work of two pilots."

"The plane is fine, Lissa. You know Leo keeps it in top running order. You'll get your license, I'll get mine, and Will can take it easy." Terry looked at her sharply. "What's wrong? You never used to worry about anything before."

"I've *always* worried, Terry. But I've tried hard not to show it."

Terry nodded his approval. "You can't spend the rest of your life brooding about life's problems. It's unhealthy, Lissa."

"That's what I thought, too," she said slowly. "I always believed that, given time, things would sort themselves out on their own."

"They usually do," Terry insisted.

"I don't know," Lissa said, uneasy now. She remembered A.J.'s accusation that she saw the world through rose-colored glasses. "Maybe hoping the bad things in life will just go away isn't enough."

"Neither is getting an ulcer over it." Terry's voice was flippant. "You'll see. Everything'll be fine."

"I hope you're right." *But this time I don't think you are.*

"That's my girl." Terry gave Lissa a thumbs-up gesture and a cheerful smile that didn't affect her at all. Instead, she had still another worry to add to her list—the influence "Rebel" Corbett was already having on her.

"CALL ME WHEN you're done, and I'll be back to pick you up," Leo said as he landed the older-model cargo plane at JeffCo for Lissa's first lesson with her new instructor.

"Okay, Leo, thanks. I'll see you then. Bye!"

Lissa fluttered her hand, jumped out of the plane and glanced at her watch. She saw that it was after ten and swore silently as she began running toward the Flight Line. Leo was a slow, methodical flyer, and he had taken much longer to reach JeffCo than Will usually did. She was going to be late for her appointment and knew she was going to hear about it.

She dashed into the lounge, the agreed-upon meeting place, and instantly spotted A.J. among the other pilots. He was dressed casually, but his bearing was stiff, his movements impatient. Lissa's excitement at the first sight of him died at the look of anger on his face. She walked reluctantly toward him.

"You're late!" A.J. snapped. "If you think I'm going to stand for this kind of nonsense from a non-paying student, you're wrong." He grabbed his clipboard and flight bag and headed for the door. "I've got some racing practice to get in. You're on your own, Miss Hannelly."

"Wait!" Lissa ran frantically after him and clutched his arm. Her strength was nothing compared to his. She was towed along in his wake, out the door and along the concrete.

"My usual pilot wasn't flying our plane! Our mechanic took me, and he practically never flies. He was so slow! I couldn't do a thing about it! I left early, I swear I did!"

A.J. stopped his determined march to his plane, Lissa still holding on for dear life. "How early?"

"We left at nine o'clock. You can call my grandmother and ask her, if you don't believe me."

A.J. studied her carefully for a moment. "All right, I'll allow your lapse this time. In the future, if you can't be here when I say, don't bother showing up at all."

Lissa glanced at the stern face. He was being unreasonable; she was only ten minutes late. But right now she was too relieved to do anything else but say, "I'll be on time, I promise."

A.J. nodded. "Tell me, Miss Hannelly. Do you always throw yourself at men when you want something?" He glanced down at her hands, still tightly clasping his arm.

Lissa dropped his arm and immediately thrust her hands behind her back. She felt her neck turn red, and when A.J. continued to hold her gaze, her cheeks followed.

"I was worried about Hannelly Air Charter!"

"Very worried, it appears. Now—" A.J. handed her his clipboard "—follow me to the plane. I want you to perform the preflight exterior check."

Lissa did, all the while fighting her embarrassment. She hoped A.J. hadn't guessed she found him...what? Attractive, certainly; infuriating, definitely. But A.J. Corbett's effect on Lissa was more than just a physical one. A.J. exposed aspects of her character she hadn't known she possessed. He released emotions inside her that had never before been tapped. Getting to know A.J. meant getting to know herself, and the combination was strangely exhilarating.

But what if A.J. thought she was throwing herself at him, offering feminine adulation—and perhaps other attentions!—in return for a good exam score? Lissa mentally writhed at the thought and resolved to concentrate on her flying instead of her instructor, a task easier said than done.

"Ready? Then climb in," A.J. ordered.

Lissa complied and started the interior instrument check. But to her surprise, A.J. took the clipboard out of her hand. The pilot was supposed to keep custody of all paperwork, and she would be flying.

"What did I do wrong?" she asked irritably.

"Nothing—so far." His lips twitched upward at her reaction to his answer. "It's time for lesson number one—be prepared."

"I know how to be prepared," Lissa asserted, folding her arms across her chest. "Being prepared means finishing the preflight check, which you stopped me from doing."

"Being prepared means being ready for all contingencies. What would you have done if I hadn't waited for you? I told you to be on time."

"For heaven's sake, I was only ten minutes late!"

"That isn't the point. You didn't allow yourself extra time to get here. There's the faulty attitude I was talking about. Pilots who don't expect the unexpected and don't plan in advance for it run into trouble. Lesson number one for today—explain how this applies to you."

Lissa knew they weren't going anywhere until she did. Besides, loath though she was to admit it, "Rebel" Corbett was right again.

"I assumed I'd get here on time and left everything to Leo."

"And?"

Lissa sighed. "I should have taken control of the situation myself, considering Leo's slow flying beforehand, and made arrangements accordingly."

"And?"

"I was wrong," she said reluctantly.

"You're learning." A.J. must have seen that he'd made his point, because he no longer belabored it. "Ready to go?" he asked. He gestured toward the dual set of controls, common in instructor planes.

A shaken Lissa made sure her voice was firm before she said, "Whenever you are."

"Okay, finish your checklist and start her up."

Lissa did as she was told, then threw him a quick glance. She wasn't doing anything else without further directions.

"I've already filed a flight plan, so get your tower instructions and let's put her in the air."

Lissa nodded, then picked up the mike and requested taxi instructions for takeoff.

The tower cleared them a runway, giving them their altimeter setting and the wind directions.

Lissa carefully maneuvered the plane down the taxiway to the runway, waiting for clearance. She didn't have long to wait.

"This is JeffCo tower. Cessna 289, you are cleared for takeoff." There was a brief pause, then, "Good luck, Rebel. You're going to need it."

Lissa bit her lip as A.J. turned her way, his eyes sparkling with amusement.

"Well, Miss Hannelly, I see your reputation has preceded you." He took the mike from her and radioed back in his deep voice, "Thanks, JeffCo. Cessna 289 out."

Lissa frowned at him, silently cursed the tower man who'd broken radio protocol to have a joke at her expense and proceeded to give everyone the sight of her best takeoff ever. She climbed steadily, lined the aircraft up at the altitude and heading A.J. ordered, then sat back for the next ten minutes and relaxed.

"You might as well wipe that smug smile off your face," A.J. finally commented. "Just because you made a fairly, and I emphasize fairly, competent takeoff doesn't mean you sit there and gloat about it."

Lissa started guiltily. That was exactly what she'd been doing.

"You should be checking your gauges to see if everything went smoothly during takeoff. Better find out now, while you're still close to home, instead of later, when you're over the Rockies with no place to land."

Lissa turned toward him, ready to argue, then closed her mouth. What could she say? He was infuriating, but he was right. She hadn't actually noticed anything wrong with the plane, but of course she should be checking the instruments periodically.

With A.J.'s eyes on her, she glanced at the gauges. She blinked in surprise and then horror as she saw the oil-gauge needle pointing dangerously low. She immediately picked up the mike to get landing instructions.

"We've got to go back," she explained frantically, keying the mike. "We've got an oil leak. I need to land before the engine freezes up!"

A.J. took the microphone from her hand. "I'll call it in."

Lissa turned the plane around in a tight bank as he asked, "Shouldn't you have checked those gauges sooner?"

She felt sweat break out on her forehead. How long could the plane fly without any oil? "Just call the tower!" she demanded. "Hurry!"

A.J. nonchalantly toyed with the microphone cord. "You didn't answer my question."

"Yes, I should have checked sooner." Lissa strained to estimate the distance to the runways far below. "Now get clearance for me to drop altitude and land, or we're going to crash!"

"Becoming hysterical isn't going to help the situation," A.J. cautioned. Lissa noticed that he didn't look worried at all, although he did pick up the mike again.

"JeffCo Tower, this is Cessna 289, over."

Lissa felt her neck muscles tighten and bunch from tension as JeffCo responded.

"JeffCo Tower, I'm twenty miles south of Golden, request landing instructions, over."

"Roger, Cessna 289, right traffic, landing runway two-nine. Altimeter is three-zero-zero-two, winds are three-zero-five at fourteen knots gusting to twenty-five."

"Roger, JeffCo. Altimeter three-zero-zero-two. Cessna 289, out." A.J. turned toward Lissa. "You're expected to repeat by individual digit all altimeter readings given while in flight. You remember that, don't you?''

"Yes," Lissa said, her voice hoarse. "You didn't call in a Mayday. You didn't ask for fire equipment."

"In my judgment, it's not an emergency yet. Just land the plane, Miss Hannelly."

Lissa felt the sweat run down her sides as she once again checked the oil gauge. It was still in the red-line danger area. She swallowed hard and heard A.J. say, "You're doing just fine, Lissa. We're almost there."

Lissa nodded once, keeping all her concentration on her flying. Why hadn't she checked that oil gauge sooner? So what if she'd had a great takeoff? She could think of better things to put on her tombstone—like death from old age, for instance. Lissa entered the downwind leg of the traffic pattern, and A.J. picked up the mike again to get final clearance.

"Okay, Lissa, let's see if your landing compares to your takeoff."

Lissa didn't care how pretty her landing was, but she nodded again and concentrated on landing safely and accurately. It wasn't until the wheels touched pavement that she let out a slow breath of relief.

"Not too bad," A.J. casually remarked as the radio crackled out taxi instructions. The operator finished with, "Cessna 289, contact ground control on one-one-nine-point-five, over."

"Roger, JeffCo. Thank you." A.J. looked at Lissa expectantly. "Well, tune in the radio to frequency 119.5. Do I have to do everything?"

With shaking fingers, Lissa forced herself to reach for the dial. She'd nearly died because of her own negligence. And she would have taken A.J. Corbett with her. Her chest tightened with guilt and dismay.

"JeffCo ground, this is Cessna 289, over," said A.J. in a calm voice.

"Cessna 289, you are cleared to taxi in front of flight operations. Welcome back, Rebel."

"Roger, JeffCo ground, out." A.J. hung up the microphone. "Okay, Lissa, park her. You know where she goes."

Lissa carefully taxied into A.J.'s designated parking area, then reached for the ignition.

"Wait a minute," A.J. said. He leaned forward and tapped once, twice, at the glass covering the oil gauge. Before Lissa's eyes the needle jerked, then moved to a perfectly acceptable oil level.

"Hmm. Seems I have a sticky oil gauge here. I'll have to get maintenance to take a look at it. I like my planes in perfect working order. Now you can shut her down. We're finished."

A.J. reached for his flight bag with one hand, tucking the clipboard under his arm. "Coming?"

"The oil gauge was *defective?*" Lissa stared at him with a slowly dawning realization. He had deliberately deceived her into thinking their lives were at risk. And she'd actually berated herself for endangering him!

"We weren't about to crash, and you knew it all along!" she accused him. She was trembling again, but this time from rage, not fear. "The gauge was defective before we took off! That's why you didn't call in a Mayday! What a dirty, underhanded trick! You nearly scared me to death!" Her fists clenched, and for a second she seriously considered hitting him.

"True," he replied. "But a student who's failed her final flight exam not once, not twice, but *four* times needs more appropriate methods of instruction."

"Appropriate? I thought we were going to crash!" Lissa screamed at him.

"That, Miss Hannelly, was the point." His voice lashed like a whip. "Most accidents happen during takeoffs and landings, and you're an accident waiting for a place to happen. You didn't pay proper attention to your instruments after takeoff. You were too busy trying to make an impression on me with your fancy flying. In the meantime, you totally ignored a red-line gauge that could actually have been trying to tell you something."

A.J. reached to open his door. "If you don't like my lessons, lady, then you'd better quit right now, because I guarantee you things will get a lot worse before they get better." He glanced at her pale face and her sweat-stained blouse. "If you quit now, all you'll have lost is your dignity and the price of a few tanks of gas."

He exited the aircraft, leaving Lissa to stay or follow him, as she pleased. Lissa felt her rage intensify, then explode. She grabbed her purse and slammed open the plane door.

"You'd just love that, wouldn't you?" she yelled at him. "Well, you're not getting rid of me that easily. No matter how many times you make a fool of me, I'm not giving up until I get certified!"

A.J. gave her a long, hard look. "Well, well, what a surprise. I thought little Miss Happy-Go-Lucky would be sobbing on my shoulder by now." Despite his sarcasm, there was a fleeting, almost begrudging hint of admiration in his voice. "But maybe you can make it to the ladies' room before the waterworks start.''

"Why, you . . .'' That was the last straw. She *would* hit him. No court in the world would convict her. She scooted out the small door and down onto the pavement, then took two steps toward him.

Lissa had overestimated her strength. The strain and tension of the past few moments had made rubber of her legs. She felt her purse slide from her hands and the ground start to tilt. It was only through sheer willpower that she kept her balance before A.J. dashed to her and supported her in his arms.

"Take it easy,'' he said, his voice husky. "I'm sorry. I didn't enjoy scaring you, but you gave me no choice. Can't you see how unprepared you are to fly a plane?''

"You were deliberately cruel,'' she whispered.

"Lissa, I had a reason. If I hadn't done it, some other examiner eventually would. We all know who the incompetent fliers are, and we all have a responsibility to get them out of the air. You're a life-threatening hazard! Accept that fact and be glad I didn't send the plane into a screaming dive, or use any of the other tactics we save for bad-risk students.''

Lissa's head was still spinning, but her answer was clear. "If you think I'm going to thank you for your *kindness,* you're sadly mistaken!''

A.J. shook his head. "Go home, Lissa Hannelly. Give it up. You'll save us both a lot of grief.''

Lissa found that her arms had wrapped themselves tightly around his neck. She gazed up at him, her eyes wide. "I can't. I won't.''

"You should, damn it,'' A.J. said. Then he kissed her, his lips hard on hers, holding nothing back.

Lissa felt his heartbeat pound against hers, or was it her heart pounding against his? All too soon, it seemed, she was abruptly pushed away from him, although his hands were still on her arms. Gradually the tilting concrete beneath her feet stabilized, and she was able to stand on her own.

"Wh-What..." Lissa stuttered, then started again. "What was that for?" she asked as A.J. finally released her.

"Just a little shock therapy for a hysterical woman," he said, but his amused smile didn't quite reach his eyes. "You should know by now that I have my own way of doing things." He bent to pick up the flight bag and clipboard he'd dropped rushing to her aid.

Lissa's body seemed to vibrate with a new awareness. And she knew her recent experience, however frightening, wasn't the only reason.

"Personally I don't think you can live through another lesson, Miss Hannelly. But if you're interested in going out with me on a social basis, I'm definitely interested."

"You're what?" Lissa couldn't believe what she was hearing.

"I'd like to take you out. Do you prefer concerts, the theater or more casual activities?"

"You're serious!"

"Of course I am. If you're no longer a student of mine, there's nothing unethical in asking you out, is there?"

Lissa drew an indignant breath. "Is that why you scared me half to death? So you could scare me away from flying and ask me out with a clear conscience?"

"No. I did it because I feel you're a menace in the sky. But that doesn't blind me to your other qualities." His smile was appreciative. "I think you'd be a very interesting woman to—"

"Dream on! The only time I'll be spending with you is in the cockpit," Lissa said emphatically. "I'm interested in having flying lessons with you—nothing else!" Lissa flushed. "I'm not interested in romance. I just turned down one proposal of marriage."

"I didn't say anything about marriage," he said bluntly.

Lissa's face grew even hotter. "Then what are you talking about?"

"I'm talking about dating. You set the pace, and you set the rules. I'll go along with whatever you want, because I think the two of us have possibilities. But I'll be honest with you, Lissa. I'm not in the market for either a cheap affair or a wife."

"And just what else is left?" Lissa asked, hiding her pleasure at the obvious interest in his eyes. She should still be angry at him for the stunt he'd pulled, not contemplating an evening as his date!

"Good clean fun. Just because you're an adult doesn't mean you can't play once in a while. Even I know that. When's the last time you simply *played*, Lissa? The last time you enjoyed yourself?"

"I—I can't remember," she was forced to admit. Lately it seemed she was always working at the business—or worrying about the business. What bliss it would be to put all thoughts of the old plane and her grandfather far away for one evening. A.J. Corbett might be just the man to show her how.

"I think you need someone like me in your life," A.J. announced.

Lissa clamped down her pleasure. "What about Alanna?" she asked suspiciously.

"Alanna and I live pretty far apart and we both date other people. I'd like to spend time with someone a little closer to home."

"I don't think I like being just a convenient option."

A.J. said nothing.

Lissa took the plunge. "But I'm not saying no, either. You teach me to fly well enough to pass. When I've got my license, we'll see."

He gave her a slow smile. "Fair enough. I'll see you tomorrow afternoon. That's two o'clock *sharp,* Lissa. Good day." He walked to the parking lot as though he hadn't a care in the world.

Lissa stood there, staring after him and feeling suddenly confused. Had he really meant to drop her as a student or only pretended so she'd agree to date him? If that was the case, she didn't know whether to be flattered or furious.

She watched him pull out of the parking lot in a flashy car built for speed. Then she retrieved her purse and walked back to the lounge to call Leo. It wasn't until her hands had stopped shaking that she found herself wondering if the trembling was from the faulty oil gauge or A.J.'s flawless kiss.

CHAPTER THREE

"LISSA, ARE YOU OKAY? You haven't touched your lunch," Margaret said with concern.

Lissa was the last one at the table; everyone else had finished and left. "I'm fine, Grandma. I'm just nervous about my next lesson." She checked her watch, intending to leave in a few minutes to make her two-o'clock appointment.

Margaret sat down beside her, smoothing the apron carefully over her lap. "Lissa, you don't have to fly if you don't want. Maybe no one else noticed, but I saw how upset you were when you came home yesterday. And today you're still a bundle of nerves. If you don't want to be a pilot, then don't be one. You know I'll back you up with your grandfather."

Lissa glanced lovingly at the tiny delicate figure of her grandmother. Behind that sweet face was a fierce uncompromising loyalty.

"Thanks, Grandma, but I want to prove that I can do it. A.J. Corbett doesn't seem to think I can." Lissa pictured A.J.'s disapproval—his patronizing voice, those mocking eyes, the fact that he was obviously waiting for her to fail. It all grated on her nerves.

Margaret gave her granddaughter a shrewd look. "Make sure you're flying for the right reasons, Lissa. You don't have to prove anything to anyone except yourself. Not to me, not your grandfather and certainly not your flight instructor. Now finish your sandwich like a good girl."

Margaret stroked Lissa's hair affectionately, changing from wise muse to doting grandmother again. Lissa ate another few bites to please her while reflecting on her words. *Was* she just trying to impress A.J.?

She was. Lissa had to be honest with herself. Though she didn't know him well, A.J.'s opinion had become important to her. She wasn't sure when that had occurred, but he was uppermost in her thoughts, even while she slept. All last night she'd had disturbing dreams of crashing a plane and killing, not herself, but A.J. Corbett.

Lissa hurried out to look for Leo, eager to get to her lessons. But she recognized that it was as much for the exhilaration of A.J.'s presence as to help the family business.

A.J. wouldn't like that, she knew. He'd accuse her of not getting her priorities straight, of indulging in a bad attitude again. Lissa frowned. All of a sudden she was sizing up her personal actions against *his* particular code. That was fine for flying, but she didn't think it was a very smart thing to do in her personal life.

A memory of his kiss flashed in her head. No, Lissa decided as she climbed into her grandfather's newer plane, it wasn't very smart at all.

Lissa was a full half hour early for her next lesson, and she waited impatiently in the lounge until A.J. arrived promptly at two. He was dressed in his usual jeans and sports shirt, sleeves rolled up to the elbows, and he carried his flight bag and clipboard.

"Hello, Lissa. I see you made it on time today," he observed in a matter-of-fact voice.

"Of course. I was even early. I wouldn't miss this lesson for the world."

"You may change your mind before the day is over," A.J. remarked, and Lissa felt her heart sink as she followed him to the Aerobat. What was he going to do to her this time?

Her takeoff was smooth, a compliment to the windless day and clear skies. It was a beautiful day for flying. Unfortunately Lissa was too busy anticipating A.J.'s next hair-raising move to enjoy much of the scenery.

After an hour of flying due south along the Continental Divide, A.J. said, "I'll take the controls for a while. You look like you could do with a rest."

"No, no. I'm fine." Lissa looked at him suspiciously. What was he up to now?

"Don't worry, I'm not up to anything," he said easily. He'd obviously read the unspoken question in her face—and just as obviously enjoyed her annoyance. "Lissa, don't ever play poker. You're too transparent."

"Excuse me, but it's hard to hide terror. I just know something awful is headed my way."

"How bad anything is depends on how you handle it. However, I *will* tell you that today's lesson is verbal."

"You mean I don't have to worry about defective oil gauges or screaming dives or any of your other stocks-in-trade?" She let him take the controls.

A.J. didn't seem offended by her sarcasm. "I'm glad to see you've begun to anticipate some of the... possibilities. That's a good sign. It means your attitude's improving. Now, do me a favor, would you? Please get the pack of gum out of my flight bag and peel me a stick."

Lissa did as he asked, holding it toward him so that he could take it into his mouth without lifting his hands from the controls. His lips brushed her fingers, and Lissa snatched her hand away.

A.J. raised one eyebrow. "I don't bite, you know. Help yourself if you want any."

"No, thanks. I never need the stuff," she said, referring to pilots' propensity for chewing gum. It helped ears pop and adjust to changing pressure better than the other methods, such as yawning or pinching one's nose and blowing hard.

"I never used to need it, either," A.J. admitted, and Lissa suddenly remembered what one of her previous instructors had told her.

"I heard about your ears."

A.J. shrugged. "I was lucky. I have negligible hearing loss. But I do have problems with pressure at higher altitudes."

There was a wistful expression in A.J.'s eyes, and Lissa said impulsively, "You miss the military, don't you?"

There was a pause, then, "Yes and no. It was a rigidly structured way of life, and I wasn't my own boss. I hated that."

"Is that how you got your code name? Rebel?"

"As a matter of fact, it was," he said, sounding surprised. "How did you find out about that?"

"Oh, someone mentioned it. So, who gave you the name?"

"My first instructor pilot."

"Did you deserve it?"

A.J. smiled and said nothing.

"What'd you do? Break every rule in the book?"

The smile grew and reached his eyes. "Not *all* of them. But when I felt I was right, especially about flying, well—" he shrugged "—I felt obliged to take a stand."

"I can imagine," Lissa said. "But you're a civilian now. You can make your own rules."

"True, but I had to pay a price. The best part of the military—what I really miss—was the great flying. It was just me and my craft, traveling over new territory. Each time I went up, I saw something different. I could go anywhere..."

"But you can still do that now," Lissa reminded him.

"It isn't the same. Military craft are carefully designed machines, with all the advances of modern technology. And the speed, Lissa—" he shook his head reverently "—the sheer grace and speed of those jets is incredible. I could fly from continent to continent and still be home in time for dinner." His eyes fired with enthusiasm, then it faded.

"But those days are gone. I'll never break the sound barrier again," he said in a calm, dispassionate voice.

"I'm sorry—" Lissa began, but A.J. firmly cut her off.

"Don't be. What's done is done, and I don't live in the past."

Lissa turned a little in her seat to watch him. It was funny how she could immediately switch her attention from flying lessons to him. But at times like these, A.J. Corbett was far more interesting than learning how to fly.

"Did you come from a military family?" she asked curiously.

"No. It's true that most people in the military have relatives who served, but I was the exception to the rule. My family's from Crested Butte. My father mined coal there while my mother stayed home to keep house and take care of me. I was her only child, but I was a handful because I was sickly and prone to accidents."

Lissa stared at the vital, muscular man beside her. "I find that hard to believe."

"Oh, it's true, all right. I was the original ninety-eight-pound weakling. I was always getting bandaged or stitched up for something."

"You?"

"Oh, yes. One summer I hurt my eye in a spitball fight with a classmate. Another year I broke a leg when I slipped on some ice. And I caught every cold and virus that came along. Mom says she doesn't know how I survived to adulthood." His voice was filled with love.

"Are your parents still living?"

A.J. nodded. "They moved to Arizona after I graduated from college. The winters were just too much for them. I fly down to Phoenix quite often."

"They must have missed you terribly when you joined the military."

"They did. But I had to get away from the old hometown. I didn't want to be a coal miner. It's a difficult, dangerous life. And a dead end, as far as I was concerned. I'm just grateful my father got out when he did, still in relatively good health." He smiled gently. "To my parents' eternal relief, I got a math scholarship from a very good college."

"Math?" Lissa echoed in surprise.

A.J.'s lips formed a wry expression. "My parents thought I'd make a good accountant."

Lissa shook her head. "I can't quite picture you locked inside an office surrounded by computer spread sheets."

"Neither could I."

"So how did you end up in the military?"

"Fate, I guess. Right after I graduated from college, a friend showed me an ad in the paper. The air force was looking for math and science majors to train as pilots, and he wanted me to drive him down to the recruiters. The more I studied that ad, the more intrigued I was. It seemed a good move, becoming a pilot. My friend decided not to sign up, but I did."

"Obviously it was the right choice."

"As it turned out. With my math abilities, navigation was a snap. So was learning all the digital cockpit instrumentation. Somewhere in my youth, I'd developed the reflexes needed to fly a plane. I never looked back. Despite my personal dislike for that structured kind of life, the military was in many ways a satisfying experience for me."

Lissa hesitated, then asked softly, "What about now?"

"I have my planes, my pylon racing and my students."

What Lissa wanted to ask was, "Aren't you lonely? Don't you ever want to settle down with a wife?" Deep inside, hardly daring to admit it, she wondered if A.J. could ever be interested in someone like her.

Instead she asked, "Is that enough?"

"I can't complain. At least I lived through the crash that ended my military career two years ago. Not everyone did." He turned toward Lissa. "Want me to tell you what happened?"

"Not if you don't want to talk about it," she replied quickly.

"Consider this today's lesson, and listen carefully."

Lissa bit her lip. Since her parents' death, she found listening to crash stories particularly painful.

"I was stationed at Luke Air Force Base in Arizona at the time. There was a pilot in distress over the mountains. He was a student of mine, and something had gone wrong with his aircraft. I remained in voice contact with him, trying to give him support, but his aircraft wouldn't respond. I ordered him to eject, but with the mechanical problems he was having, it was impossible. His cartridges were faulty. They wouldn't fire the canopy off the cockpit."

A.J. checked his heading, made a slight correction, then continued. "The student finally lost control and crashed in the hills. And then we lost all power ourselves." He shook his head, remembering.

"Can you imagine the odds of two planes breaking down like that at once? It was unbelievable."

Lissa took a deep breath. "A.J., I don't think I want to hear the end of this story."

He gave her a glance that said, "Afraid?" and went on, anyway.

"There we were in a flat spin, and I couldn't get out of it. My student was flying solo, but I wasn't. I had an R.I.O.—a radar intercept officer—with me. I told him we had to eject. During that procedure, my eardrums ruptured, and that was the end of my career."

"What about your radar man?" Surely he was fine. Lissa couldn't quite bring herself to ask about the student.

For a moment, A.J.'s hands tensed on the controls. "I gave him plenty of notice, but he didn't tuck his head down when we ejected. It's established procedure, and he should have remembered. He broke his neck."

"Oh, no." Lissa was horrified.

"Yes. We went through flight school together, too." His voice was harsh with the memory of a lost friend.

"I..." Her own voice caught. She knew better than anyone what it was like to lose a loved one to the skies. "And the student?" She had to know.

"He crash-landed, but walked away from the site alive. My R.I.O. was buried with full military honors. The victim survived, and the rescuer died."

Lissa felt her throat tighten with emotion as A.J. turned to face her again.

"It just goes to prove, Lissa, that the right attitude can make all the difference, even in the worst situations."

Silence. Then she whispered, "I'm ready to take over the controls now."

The handoff was made. Shaken, Lissa sat quietly, concentrating on her flying. She decided she preferred being instructed by faulty oil gauges than by A.J.'s stories. Slowly she began to calm down. The mountains were to the west of them, but A.J. told her to climb higher, and soon she could see down to their rugged bases. The aspens that gave Golden its name were clothed in summer green instead of their fall glory, while the evergreens were lush and full, with no winter winds to tear at their boughs.

After a while A.J. spoke again. "Would you like to see some Pueblo Indian ruins?"

Lissa looked at him in surprise. "I beg your pardon?"

"I thought we'd fly down to the Four Corners area, toward Mesa Verde. There's no easy place to land, but we can fly over the ruins, then head west over the mountains. I'll take you back home today so you don't have to wait for Leo."

Lissa felt a warm glow. "You're offering me a bona fide scenic tour *and* a ride home? Mr. Corbett, are you actually trying to be nice to me?"

"Bite your tongue. I have a reputation to maintain," he said with a straight face. "I'm never nice to my students. Remember that. Now let me have the controls again."

Lissa complied, but she could see that A.J. was uncomfortable with her gratitude. She smiled ever so slightly. If he was trying to hide a soft heart, he wasn't doing a very good job of it. But she'd go along with the game.

"I can take anything you dish out. You won't see me crying on your shoulder."

A.J.'s deep voice rippled with amusement. "I see that earlier remark of mine offended you. My apologies, Miss Hannelly."

"You've been calling me Lissa," she reminded him. "And I'd love to see the ruins."

"Then look sharp, because we're almost there. Watch along the insides of the cliffs for them—they're called Cliff Palace. I can't fly too low along these formations, but I can get you close enough for a quick peek."

He turned the Cessna in a long lazy bank and circled the cliffs. "Hold on tight, and don't worry about the plane. Just look."

"There they are!" The orange adobe ruins came into view. "I can see them!" Lissa's hands splayed against the window in excitement.

"Aren't they great? Best preserved ruins in the United States. Hard to believe that people settled here at Mesa Verde almost two thousand years ago."

"Oh, I can't see anymore." Lissa couldn't hide her disappointment; the plane's pass had taken them by the ruins all too briefly.

Lissa missed the smile A.J. gave her. "No problem. We can circle by again."

"Can we?" she asked eagerly.

A.J. nodded and swung over the top of Mesa Verde. Its name, "green table," came from the thick forest of green juniper and piñon trees that covered the summit. He banked again, and once more Lissa's window faced out on the orange adobe of the ruined cliff dwellings.

"Look at them! There must be a hundred rooms!"

"Actually, Cliff Palace has over two hundred. There are smaller cliff dwellings around, too, but they aren't as easy to see by air. You have to go in on foot."

Lissa kept craning her head to look back as A.J. turned the Cessna to a northeast heading and started out toward Hannelly Air Charter. "Thank you," she said, her face beaming with pleasure. "It was beautiful."

"Well, I can't teach you much when you're all tensed up and waiting for me to spring another dastardly deed. I had to relax you somehow."

"You mean this was just an instructor's exercise in psychology?" Lissa was torn between feelings of dismay and disbelief. "I thought you were trying to be ... nice."

"Heaven forbid. One more word about how *nice* I am, and I'll have to charge you double what you're paying now."

Lissa grinned, suddenly feeling lighthearted. "But I'm not paying you anything, am I?"

A.J. responded with a change of subject, but his voice was friendly. "Are you ready to take the controls again? I've set the heading for your runway."

Lissa took over. The conversation during the rest of the trip was strictly lesson-related, but Lissa found it difficult to keep her mind on flying. A.J.'s presence was proving to be more and more of a distraction. The two of them sat inches apart in a cozy space far from the rest of the world. She concentrated on A.J.'s strict coaching, but she still was aware of his nearness. Aware of his strong, capable hands, his deep blue eyes and determined chin, his scent. Fighting that sensation was as difficult as any flight lesson had ever been.

Despite her inner turmoil, she managed to proceed to Hannelly Air Charter without further incident and land at her grandfather's runway.

"I need to gas up," A.J. said, eyeing the gauge. "Can I purchase some fuel from you?"

Lissa had already anticipated him. "We're headed there right now," she said as she taxied the plane slowly toward the pumps. "But the gas is on the house. After all, you aren't charging me for lessons."

"I'll pay. Can I pump my own?"

Lissa nodded, watching him jump out and do just that. He had given her such pleasure by taking her to

Mesa Verde, and yet he'd refused her offer of free fuel. It wouldn't have hurt him to let her return a favor, she thought. But she could still make it up to him in other ways; besides, she wasn't ready to see him leave yet.

"Can you stay for dinner?" Lissa asked as she joined him outside.

"It's getting late," A.J. replied, but with enough reluctance that Lissa insisted.

"You're instrument-rated. You can fly home in the dark. I'd like you to meet my grandmother. We're so isolated here, she loves meeting new people." *And I'd like to concentrate on you without having to worry about my lessons.* "Please."

"In that case, I'd be honored. Maybe later you could show me around. I'd like to see your planes."

"We can do that right now if you want. Ours aren't half as nice as yours," Lissa warned him, "although they can carry a heavy cargo load and eight passengers."

"That sounds impressive. Lead the way."

They crossed the grassy area between the main house and the small hangar. Lissa gestured him inside with a flourish. "Here they are," she announced as they stepped inside. "Our mechanic keeps them in pretty good running order."

A.J. studied the polished surface of the nearest plane and ran his hands along its side.

"Want to kick the tires?" Lissa asked with amusement.

A.J. ignored her humor and continued his inspection. "She looks pretty old," he finally said. "I'd be a little nervous flying her in poor conditions."

"We usually take the newer plane in bad weather and try to use the older model for the shorter, less strenuous hops."

A.J. walked over to the other plane with its gleaming metal and sparkling trim. "This is more like it." His words echoed off the hangar ceiling. "How old is this one? Three, four years?"

"Seven, actually," Lissa said proudly, knowing the plane didn't look it, thanks to Leo's expert care. "And she flies like a dream."

A.J. looked from the newer plane to the other one. "That older model should be retired."

"I wish we could. But we'd lose our bid with the ranger station if we had only one plane. The contract requires two planes and two pilots to handle the workload. The older plane will have to do for now."

A.J. shook his head, a grim expression on his face. "You can't afford to fly with shoddy equipment."

"Our planes aren't shoddy! We have them on a regular maintenance schedule, and they fly just fine."

"The older one is outdated!" A.J. exclaimed. "Here's another perfect example of your poor attitude."

"I don't want to hear another word about my attitude!" Lissa warned, her eyes sparking dangerously.

"You're going to, anyway. Good pilots don't imperil their own lives and those of their passengers. Flying in antiquated equipment is asking for trouble. You couldn't pay me to get into that bucket of bolts!"

Lissa sucked in her breath at the insult. "I know the plane is old. And yes, I'm sure it'll need to be retired eventually. But it's hardly a ... a flying coffin!"

"I wonder." A.J. gave the older craft a look of scorn. "I'd run, not walk, to the nearest aircraft dealer and buy another one today."

"I'll have you know both planes have passed all their government inspections. And not all of us can make enough money pylon racing to pay for our airplanes," Lissa threw back at him.

A.J. strode closer until he was just a few inches away from her. "There are such things as banks. You already have one new plane. Is it paid for?"

"Yes."

"Good. So use it for collateral and take out another loan for a second craft."

"We did offer it, but we couldn't get another loan. Grandfather tried."

A.J. looked skeptical. "I can't believe that. How did you get the newer plane in the first place?"

"I don't want to talk about it."

Lissa turned her back on him to walk away, but A.J. grabbed her arm and whirled her around.

"How did you get the newer plane?" he repeated.

Lissa bit her lip, then answered. "The insurance people replaced the previous one."

"What previous plane?" A.J. demanded.

"I don't have to tell you our personal business," Lissa retorted, trying to pull free.

"Tell me, Lissa. *Now*. I'm not leaving until you do," he threatened. "I mean it. What previous plane?"

"The one my parents were flying." Tears started to gather, but Lissa forced them back.

A.J.'s face filled with grim determination, and his hands tightened on her shoulders. "What happened to the original plane?"

She gave no answer, but her silence spoke as loudly as words.

"It crashed?"

"Yes." Lissa swallowed hard. "They were the only ones on board."

"I'm sorry. I didn't know." He was silent a moment, then gently asked, "Can you tell me if their plane was the same age as this older model?"

Again Lissa gave a barely perceptible nod. She was *not* going to cry, she told herself.

A.J. sighed heavily. "I suppose the crash was caused by mechanical failure." It was a statement, not a question.

"I don't know." She raised her eyes to his in mute anguish, and now the tears spilled down her cheeks despite her best efforts. "We never found a trace of them, or the plane."

A.J. pulled her close, and Lissa didn't resist. She rested her forehead on his chest.

"I didn't want to fall apart like this." She hastily rubbed at her face, struggling to get her emotions under control.

He stroked her hair. "It's okay."

"No, it's not. I mean, I know they're dead. I've accepted it. I just wish we could find them..." Her words trailed off as she thought of a year-round snow on the higher peaks, and how it effectively blanketed everything from sight.

They stood there in a loose embrace. Lissa instinctively felt that he was remembering his R.I.O., who had died in Arizona. She knew he must think of him often, as she did of her parents. For the first time in her life, she found someone besides her grandmother who understood exactly how she felt.

"I think under the circumstances I'll pass on that meal," A.J. said quietly. He pulled gently away from her. "Would you walk me out?"

"Sure." Lissa was in no mood to eat either, now. She followed him out of the dimly lit hangar into the full brilliant sunshine. Side by side, they strolled toward A.J.'s plane.

He performed his preflight check while she silently watched. When he was finished he dated his log, then signed it.

"When is my next lesson?" she asked.

A.J. opened his plane door and threw in his clipboard before giving her an answer. "I don't want to instruct you anymore."

"What?" Lissa's mouth dropped open in surprise. "I thought I was improving. Why are you dropping me?"

"Because of your parents, Lissa. Because your parents died in a plane crash."

"I don't understand," she said in confusion. "What does that have to do with my lessons?

"Don't you see? They went out in a craft that, along with its present-day counterpart, should have been retired ages ago! They should have *known* flying that plane was risky."

"But they didn't think anything would happen!" Lissa protested.

"That's just the point," he snapped. "They didn't think. The Hannellys with their rose-colored glasses strike again. And now you have the same attitude they did. Your mechanic may be good, but he doesn't have a magic wand. I could justify keeping you on as a student if you believed the old plane should be retired immediately. But you don't. You're actually willing to wait."

"It has a few good years left. Grandfather has the paperwork that says so," Lissa stammered, her chest uncomfortably tight. If A.J. wouldn't teach her, what excuse would she have to see him again?

"That paperwork won't keep it in the air. Damn it, Lissa, I don't want to read about your death in an airplane crash and know I was the one who certified you!"

Lissa stared at him in shocked silence.

"I'm leaving."

"A.J., wait!"

"Why? So you can tell me how much you need your license? Forget it. You're the last person in the world who should have one. And if you think that you can plea-bargain for my services, you're very wrong."

"I'm not going to beg for my license." Lissa lifted her chin with determination. "But I *am* going to ask for something else. I—I've been worried about that plane, and my grandfather, for some time now," she blurted out. There was a strange sense of relief in finally forcing the truth to the surface, in finally admitting what she'd tried to ignore for so long. She went on, the words tumbling out in a headlong rush. "I haven't wanted to believe that...that they died because the plane was faulty. And I don't know enough about flying to know the true state of affairs, but I need to. I don't want anyone else dead. Will you help me?"

A.J. stopped in his tracks, staring at her, his eyes narrowed. "Lissa, are you serious?"

"I am. If you don't want to teach me anymore, that's your decision. But if you're right about that old plane..." Her voice threatened to break. "I can't stand by and let what happened to my parents happen again."

"I can't, either." A.J. ran his hand through his hair. "I get the shakes thinking about your grandfather, and the gambles he's taking—with other people's lives, including yours. I ought to report him to the FAA and let them look into it. I don't believe he'll change overnight because of anything I can say."

"But he might believe what *I* have to say, A.J. If you convince me, then I'll convince him. I want to be the one to tell him he's wrong. He deserves to hear it from family, not some outsider."

"And I'm an outsider, Lissa?" A.J. asked very softly.

Not to me. "You are to him. Please, A.J., give him a chance. He hardly ever uses the old plane now. And . . . and you could be wrong."

"There's a slim chance of that—a very slim chance."

"Then help me! Please?"

They stared at one another for a long time. A.J. sighed, shaking his head. "I'll think about it while I'm gone."

"Gone?"

"Yes, I'm flying out of town this weekend to practice at a pylon course."

Lissa's face fell at the thought of a whole weekend without seeing him. "When will you be back?"

"Probably Monday. I'll let you know what I've decided them."

Lissa watched him climb into the Cessna, but he didn't close the door.

"In the meantime, I want you to do one thing for me," A.J. said as he fastened his seat belt.

"What?"

"Stay out of that older plane, at least until I know how safe it really is."

"Isn't that a bit premature?"

"Promise me," he demanded harshly. "Now."

"I won't ride in it. You have my word."

A.J. nodded, and some of the harshness left his face. "Goodbye, Lissa." He closed the door, and after a moment the plane roared to life, then taxied down the runway.

Lissa watched the nose lift gracefully, the rest of the plane following. It wasn't until the Aerobat was a tiny speck in the sky that the words "Hurry back" fell softly from her lips.

CHAPTER FOUR

"GRANDPA, DON'T YOU think we should retire this old plane?"

Everyone was outside in the bright afternoon sun, equipped with the buckets, hoses and suds needed to wash down the two aircraft. Lissa hosed some loose grass off her bare feet, then proceeded to slap a soapy sponge on a metal wing.

"The old plane is fine. I've told you that a million times." Will's voice was rough with irritation.

"Yeah, Lissa, what's the problem?" Terry rinsed the area Leo had just scrubbed down. "You've been harping about the old model all weekend. What gives?"

"I'm just worried, that's all. A.J. says—"

Terry splashed his sponge into his bucket with a viciousness that didn't go unnoticed by anyone. "I am sick to death of hearing what A.J. Corbett says. You've had a few lessons with the guy, and all of a sudden he's the world's authority on everything."

"He may be a good pilot, Lissa, but he knows nothing about our business," Will stated firmly. He reached for the thermos of coffee Margaret had just brought out. "This old plane has a lot more years left in her."

"Maybe Lissa's right," Margaret ventured. "What do you think, Leo?"

Leo's lined face moved from Margaret to Will. "I do my best to keep her in good running order," he said cautiously.

"There, you see?" Will announced. "Leo's not worried, and neither am I."

"Maybe you should be," Lissa protested. "I was worried about the older plane long before A.J. said anything." She took a deep breath. "If I get my license, I refuse to fly it."

Terry actually dropped his hose, while Will's face turned a fearful red. "I beg your pardon, Lissa?"

"I won't fly the old plane," Lissa repeated. "I don't think it's safe."

"It's just fine for your grandfather and it was just fine for me!" Terry burst out. "What's the matter? This plane isn't good enough for you since you've been flying in Andrew Corbett's fancy model?"

Lissa looked at Terry in surprise. She had expected opposition from her grandfather, but not from him.

"I think Lissa may be right," Margaret interrupted softly. "The other plane was old, too, and my son never came back with it. I'm happy to hear that I won't have to worry about my granddaughter." Her voice wavered, and she turned abruptly, hurrying back to the house.

"Now see what you've gone and done?" Will said angrily. He walked around the airplane and began washing the other side.

"Maybe you should find yourself another instructor. You seem too easily influenced by this Corbett," Terry said, closing ranks.

Lissa felt betrayed. She'd known Terry for seven years, and she didn't like seeing this side of him at all. Was he only pleasant and cooperative because he adhered to that unrealistic attitude A.J. was so critical of? Was he only cheerful when she didn't oppose him? Lissa shivered at the thought. Thank goodness she'd never agreed to an engagement.

"Leo?" Lissa asked in a shaky voice. Leo was her friend. He wouldn't lie to her.

"I warned your grandfather the last time—"

"That's enough, Leo," Will growled.

Leo gave Lissa a sad look, then went back to his chores.

"Go check on your grandmother," Will ordered.

"I'm not going to change my mind," were Lissa's parting words before she hurried into the house.

Margaret was nowhere to be seen, so Lissa went upstairs to shower and change out of her work clothes. She put on some clean, comfortable pants and a blouse, grabbed a light jacket and headed outside for a walk. Perhaps some fresh air might settle her jumpy nerves. She'd spent the weekend hoping A.J. wouldn't cancel her lessons and fretting about the old plane and her grandfather's stubbornness.

Lissa still hadn't heard if A.J. had reported them to the FAA. She didn't want that to happen, and yet... She didn't want to fail as a pilot, either, but a sneaky little voice told her that if she did, A.J. would be free to date her. Lissa knew that kind of thinking was dangerous. She couldn't afford to give up on becoming a pilot, at least not without a fight; her family was counting on her.

But she didn't think she could give up A.J. without a fight either. He was becoming too big a part of her life. Terry and Will were right to be suspicious.

The sun's warmth was already starting to fade as Lissa reached the end of the cleared area at the edge of the forest. She put on her jacket against the coolness and began to walk briskly. The path through the shadowy woods was well-worn. There weren't many other places to get away from Hannelly Air Charter unless you drove or flew far and long.

Uncomfortably Lissa remembered her grandfather's skeptical attitude. He'd always been able to sway her before, but just lately, she'd begun to rebel. Since A.J. had started instructing her, she'd been questioning everything and everyone, including herself. So far, it hadn't been a very pleasant process.

A sleeping owl, disturbed by her presence, spread its wings and left the shaded recesses of a large Douglas fir. Lissa felt the sudden waft of air as the noiseless wings swept by. She shivered for no reason, then hurried into the brighter area farther ahead. Her life had been turned topsy-turvy. She hated being so confused and miserable one moment, so expectant and happy the next.

A.J. Corbett had opened her eyes to more than just her attitude problem. She felt aware of herself as a woman in a way she never had before. She'd become avidly curious about the future's possibilities—a future with A.J.... She'd even given her former examiner a courtesy call to let him know she'd secured A.J.'s services as an instructor, then shamelessly pumped him for information. She found the subject of A.J. Corbett extremely compelling.

The examiner confirmed A.J.'s family history, successful racing background and well-off financial status. He also added that A.J. wasn't married, had never been married and wasn't seeing anyone regularly. Lissa wanted to ask about Alanna, the woman at the ranger station, but she didn't have the nerve.

Instead, she learned that A.J. preferred casual dating to being tied down and treated his social companions with courtesy and generosity. According to the examiner, even his ex-girlfriends still pursued him. A.J. hadn't married because he preferred the excitement of racing to the restrictions of domestic life. Plenty of women had tried for an engagement ring, but no one had yet succeeded.

Lissa felt a slight pang of envy as she continued her walk. A.J. traveled to new places and met new people, and all she'd seen in twenty-five years was the same old buildings and the same few people. It was astonishing that A.J. was even interested in her. She wondered if he'd like her more if she led an exciting life, then chided herself for feeling so restless. It was bad enough to be stirring up trouble here at home; she didn't need to start daydreaming about improbable romances. But she couldn't seem to help herself. She was lonely, and somehow Terry and her family couldn't fill the void she felt inside.

Maybe once she was certified for commercial flying, she could concentrate on her social life. *If* A.J. Corbett hadn't reported Hannelly Air Charter to the FAA.

Lissa kicked at a small branch that had fallen on the path, then rounded the bend and glanced up in surprise.

"Grandma?"

"Hello, Lissa." Margaret sat quietly on an old log, her face lifted to the sun.

"I don't see you out here very often." Lissa sat down beside her grandmother.

"Oh, I come out here from time to time. Sometimes I need a change of scenery."

Lissa balanced easily on the log and drew her knees up under her chin. "I know the feeling. At least I can get away in the planes. You don't do much of that."

Margaret shook her head, the sun highlighting the silver in her hair. "I never had much heart for flying after Nathan and Rose disappeared."

Lissa looked at her grandmother with sudden insight. "You don't want me to be a pilot, do you?"

Margaret smiled, but it was a sad smile. "No, I suppose I don't. I worry about you, Lissa. You're such a trusting little thing. Whatever your parents told you to do, you did. And that holds true for your grandfather, and me, and even Terry. You always seem to think that everyone else knows what's best for you."

"Not lately I haven't," Lissa said.

Margaret nodded, and the two women sat in companionable silence for a while, soaking up the sun's warmth.

"I'm not your mother, Lissa, but I know she'd want you to live your life to its fullest. It's time you had your own plans, your own dreams. Today you finally stood up for yourself. I don't know the reason, but I was glad to see it. Maybe I won't have to worry so much about you, after all."

Lissa set her feet back down on the soft, mulchy ground and put her arm gently around her grandmother's shoulders. "I don't want you to worry about me."

"I can't help it." Margaret sighed. "I guess I should be getting back to fix dinner. You know your grandfather. He likes his meals prompt."

"I'll fix it if you want some more time to be by yourself," Lissa offered. She quickly rose, so her grandmother wouldn't refuse. "Dinner will be ready on time. I'll see you then." She leaned down to give the wrinkled petal-soft cheek a kiss.

As Lissa headed toward the path again, Margaret called her back. "Lissa, do you really mean it?"

She turned to look at her grandmother in surprise. "About cooking dinner?"

"No, about staying out of that old plane."

"I mean it."

Margaret paused, then added, "Perhaps if your father had done the same, he might be alive today."

Lissa stared at the older woman in horror. "What are you saying, Grandma?"

"Old is old, Lissa. Everything wears out sooner or later, whether it's people or planes. I ought to know." She turned her face away in a gesture of dismissal, and after a few shocked minutes, Lissa stumbled off.

Did her grandmother believe that mechanical error was the cause of the crash that killed her parents? Lissa didn't want to cause her more pain by dredging up the old tragedy. But then she thought of A.J. and the rose-colored glasses he said she wore. She'd taken a stand—not for him, but for herself. She couldn't back down now.

When Lissa returned to the house, there was a message on the answering machine from A.J. She was to be at JeffCo tomorrow morning at seven. He wouldn't report Hannelly Air Charter to the Federal Aviation Administration as long as the old plane wasn't airborne, and he intended to keep on instructing her. She felt her knees go weak with relief as she heard the message.

"Thank you," she said aloud as she rewound the tape. She prepared dinner with a lighter heart.

The next morning Lissa was up bright and early so Leo could fly her to JeffCo in the newer plane. She wanted to make sure he dropped her off with time to spare, but to her surprise A.J.'s plane was parked on Hannelly Air Charter's runway.

As Lissa hurried toward the runway, she saw that A.J. was outside, talking to her grandmother.

The conversation broke off abruptly when Lissa reached them. "Good morning, Lissa."

"Hi, Grandma. Good morning, A.J. What are you doing here? Leo was just about to take me to JeffCo."

"I thought I'd pick you up myself today. I wanted to meet Mrs. Hannelly in person. I didn't get a chance the other day."

"Oh." Lissa looked at her grandmother curiously, but Margaret averted her head. "Grandma, are you all right?"

"I'm fine." Margaret's voice came out strangely husky, almost as if she was upset. "I have to go." And she hurried back to the house.

"What's wrong?" Lissa immediately asked A.J. "What did you say to her?"

"We were just talking about your parents."

"Oh." That would explain it. "In the future, please don't bring up that subject with Grandma. It's very painful for her."

A.J. nodded. "I'm sure it is for all of you."

"Yes, well…it's harder for her. It's easier for a child to accept a parent's death than the other way around."

There was an awkward silence, which A.J. ended by remarking, "I hope you have a warm coat." He was dressed in casual outdoor clothes with sturdy boots, and carried a leather aviator's jacket. "I want to fly up to the ranger station today."

Lissa felt a sudden rush of jealousy. He'd said right from the start that he'd teach her for Alanna's sake. But Lissa resolved to not let it disturb her. She might not have had much practice at this man-woman stuff, but she vowed to hold her own with the unseen competition.

"I'm ready for whatever you have planned," she said with outward calm. "And I want to thank you for not dismissing me as a student, or reporting my grandfather's plane."

"Don't thank me yet. I'll do both if you or your grandfather step out of line. Shall we go?"

Once in the air, Lissa carefully kept watch on her instruments and her location. The oil-gauge needle had been repaired, she noticed. Knowing A.J., she fully expected him to pull some other trick, and she was determined to be ready. In fact, she even welcomed the opportunity; if she was equal to any task he set her, he'd *have* to approve of her attitude—and her . . .

"You're awfully quiet today," A.J. noted once they were well out of the JeffCo airspace and over the mountains. "Does that mean you're concentrating?"

Lissa gave him a quick glance, then said tartly, "Isn't that what you want?"

A.J. leaned back in his seat. "What I'd like is some company, if it won't distract you from your flying."

Lissa checked her instruments, then visually checked her position. "I won't let it. How was your weekend?"

"Good. I've found some interested sponsors for an upcoming race. I flew some fast laps for them and they seemed quite pleased. How was yours?"

"I've had better. I was wondering where I would ever find another flight instructor and trying to get up enough nerve to tell my grandfather why I needed one. What made you change your mind?" she asked suddenly.

A.J. shrugged. "Well, your attitude shows improvement. *Some* improvement," he amended. "Maybe there's hope for you."

"And maybe you'll get to see more of Alanna if you keep me on," Lissa said under her breath.

A.J. lifted one eyebrow at her words, and she could have bitten her tongue.

"I don't care what your motives are, as long as you keep teaching me," she replied quickly. It wouldn't do to let him think she was jealous....

She decided to add another thousand feet to her altitude. The peaks ahead were hidden by clouds, and although the maps gave their height, it was wise to allow extra margin for error.

A.J. noticed her action. "I'll do that. Let me have the controls." Under his guidance, Lissa's gentle climb changed to a steep, heavily throttled one. Then he leveled out the plane for a straight, even flight.

"There we are. Plenty of space to practice our next maneuver." He decreased the airspeed and pulled back on the stick to lift the plane's nose.

The aircraft shuddered. It was no longer flying smoothly.

"You—you've stalled the plane!" Lissa gasped, referring to the lack of lift under the wings, even though the engine itself was still working.

"That's right, I did. Get her out of it," A.J. ordered. "We're sinking fast."

Lissa threw him one agonized look, then grabbed the controls. What did the textbooks say? Oh, yes, she had to increase the airspeed to get back their lift. To do that, she had to let the plane do exactly what it was doing now—and that was falling. She pushed the stick forward, pointing the nose even farther downward. The airspeed increased drastically as the plane plummeted.

Lissa's upper lip beaded with sweat as she thought of the jagged peaks below them, but she continued to let the plane sink until she felt a change in the craft's buoyancy. She had lift once more! Gradually she pulled back on the stick as she increased her throttle. It wouldn't do to level out the plane too quickly. At their present airspeed it would unduly stress the metal. They might even stall again.

She pulled back a little, then a little more, and finally the plane felt level. She quickly checked her instruments, then opened the throttle and lifted the nose, guiding the plane up and away from those granite summits.

It wasn't until a few tense moments later that she was able to draw in a ragged breath. She turned furiously on A.J. "My previous instructors *always* practiced stalls away from the mountains and at much higher altitudes."

A.J. clearly wasn't affected by her anger. "In real life, very few unexpected stalls happen over flat fields with altitude to spare."

"But the mountains were so close! What if I couldn't recover from the stall?"

"I made sure you had plenty of room before I stalled the plane," was the calm answer. "And I was prepared to take over if you froze. Besides, the Rockies are great motivators."

"How dare you?" Lissa was shaking now, barely able to keep her hands steady on the stick.

"I had my reasons. Tell me, how many other practice stalls have you recovered from?"

Lissa refused to speak. The answer to that was zero. She'd never mastered the art before.

"I'm guessing none. Am I right?" A.J. pressed.

Lissa clenched her teeth.

"I'm waiting for an answer."

"Yes, you're right. There, are you satisfied?" she snapped.

"I certainly am. After all, that was a nice piece of work I just witnessed."

Lissa's anger diffused at the compliment. "You're satisfied with my flying?" She found her tension uncoiling despite her ordeal.

"I was this time."

At A.J.'s smile, Lissa felt a strange sensation wash through her. It was new, it was different, but it was absolutely lovely. She was trying to analyze it when A.J. spoke.

"Lissa, are you all right? You look strange."

Lissa laughed nervously. "Adrenaline letdown, I suppose. You really put me through my paces back there."

"That's what I'm here for. Let me have the controls. I'll bring us down to the ranger station runway. Take a breather."

"I'm fine," she said, but she didn't insist on retaining control of the plane. "Believe it or not," she said when her heart had stopped pounding, "I'm glad you kept me on as a student."

"I might still send you packing," A.J. warned, but his voice was kind.

"Not without my pilot's license, you won't," Lissa instantly replied.

"I'll give you credit, Lissa. You don't give up easily, do you?" A.J. reached out and gently rested his hand on her shoulder.

Lissa ached to place her hand on his, but she resisted the urge. Despite their physical and sometimes emotional closeness, she had to maintain a professional distance during lessons.

So she let her hands remain where they were and said, "I can fight for what I really want."

"And what's that, Lissa?"

You. The thought sprang from a place deep inside her. Lissa swallowed, then replied lightly, "You'd be surprised."

A.J. didn't follow up on that remark, and the rest of the flight passed uneventfully. Before long they were at the ranger station's tiny airfield—a bumpy dirt runway squeezed in where the mountains allowed. With Hannelly Air Charter's clearance, they were able to land with no problem.

A.J. stepped out first, and for the first time in their acquaintance, he gave her a hand down. Lissa's pleasure in his action was short-lived, however, for she noticed that his attention was focused on a woman approaching on horseback. She was tall and willowy, and she made Lissa, with her shorter curving figure, feel positively dumpy.

"Hello, there!" the woman called out, one hand waving cheerfully while the other easily maintained control of the cantering horse.

A.J. hurried to the edge of the makeshift runway and caught the woman as she hurled herself out of the saddle and into his arms.

"Hello, Alanna." He swung her off her feet, despite the reins in her hands and the nervous horse, then kissed her on the cheek.

"Andrew James, you pain! I didn't know until just now that you were coming. Why didn't you call?"

A.J. set Alanna down, slipping his arm around her waist with a familiarity Lissa found disconcerting.

"Well, I wasn't sure if I could make it or not. This is really a business trip. I'm instructing Lissa here." He waved a hand toward Lissa, who still stood beside the plane.

"Oh." Alanna studied Lissa closely, then brushed back a long strand of glossy hair. "Haven't we met before?"

"Clever girl," A.J. said, giving Alanna a friendly clap on the shoulder. "Yes, this is Lissa Hannelly. She's with your charter service."

"Now I remember. I've seen you ride in with the supplies." Alanna gave Lissa a welcoming smile, then held out her hand. "Pleased to meet you. I'm Alanna Stevens."

Lissa nodded and returned the handshake with rather less enthusiasm. "Hello."

Alanna brushed a kiss across A.J.'s face, then unwrapped the reins from her hand. "I have to take this horse back to the corral. Why don't I meet you at the canteen? I'll buy you both a cup of coffee," she offered.

"Sounds great. We'll meet you there," A.J. agreed.

Alanna sprang up into the saddle, clucked to her horse and was off in a cloud of dust.

"What a woman," A.J. said fondly as Alanna galloped away.

"Is she always so... energetic?" Lissa asked, hating the easy intimacy between A.J. and the other woman.

"That's Alanna for you. She never sits still."

"How did you meet her?"

"She's the daughter of an old Air Force buddy of mine, Wayne Stevens. We were once stationed together. Now Wayne's retired and he's in charge of the ranger station's helicopters. His wife died when Alanna was still in school, so when Wayne was hired six years ago, Alanna came, too."

"I'm surprised she's stayed." Especially with A.J. so far away in Golden.

"She likes it here. Come on."

The ranger-station canteen held a good crowd of people, most of them in uniform. Alanna was already seated and waved them over.

"Isn't she a ranger?" Lissa asked curiously, since Alanna wasn't dressed in the ranger greens.

"No. She's responsible for the stables. The horses were in pretty bad shape until she came along. They were rarely ridden in the winter and had no stamina at all. Now, thanks to her efforts, every single one is a good dependable ride."

"Oh." That sounded pretty impressive, at least compared with Lissa's present job as odd-jobs woman at Hannelly Air Charter.

They joined Alanna, who positively beamed with happiness at A.J.'s presence. "It's been a long time, Andrew James," she said.

A.J. smiled back, obviously just as delighted. "Too long, Alanna, but the racing circuit keeps me pretty busy this time of year."

"Yes, I know. In fact, you're usually too busy racing to instruct." She studied Lissa with renewed interest. "You must be someone very special, Miss Hannelly."

Lissa felt a blush creep up her cheeks. "Oh, no. Don't get the wrong idea. A.J. only took me on so that he could see more of you," was her honest reply.

Alanna burst into laughter. "I hardly think Andrew would give up his racing just to see the daughter of an old flying buddy. You must be underestimating yourself."

Lissa looked from Alanna to A.J. in confusion. "But you told me you wanted clearance to land here."

"A.J. and my father were in the military together. Dad was A.J.'s first instructor pilot. He gives him clearance to land whenever he wants," Alanna said. "Didn't A.J. tell you?"

"But—" That was strange. She thought that A.J.'s getting clearance to land was his main reason for taking her on as a student.

"Lissa, I said you were a challenge to my abilities as an instructor," A.J. said, observing her confusion. "Though, of course, I do enjoy the fringe benefits of spending extra time with my friends."

"That's not what I remember you saying," Lissa insisted.

A.J. shrugged. "Your memory must be having a small lapse. Alanna, how's your father?" It seemed to Lissa that A.J. was deliberately changing the subject.

"Not so good." Alanna dimpled. "I've found the man I want to marry, and Dad doesn't know what to make of it."

"Congratulations! Am I invited to the wedding?"

"Of course. You and Lissa both."

Lissa's relief overrode her curiosity about A.J.'s deception. To think that she had actually been feeling jealous of a family friend who was engaged to someone else!

"So, A.J., when are you going to decide that women are more appealing than airplanes?" Alanna gave Lissa a speculative look.

"It's hard to say. I haven't found a woman yet who doesn't want me to give up racing once she gets wedding fever."

"It's true," Alanna told Lissa. "Women flock to him in droves, but every time he starts seeing someone seriously, it always ends the same way. It seems they're all worried he'll smash himself into a million pieces."

"I hate it," A.J. said irritably. "It's bad enough having my parents worry. But ever since I started racing, every woman I meet seems to be anticipating my funeral."

"They all want him to settle down and get some nine-to-five job, like maybe a vacuum-cleaner salesman," Alanna teased.

"That'll be the day," A.J. said dryly.

"Someday you'll find the perfect woman. Maybe you have already." Alanna sent Lissa a meaningful smile. With a frankness that spoke of longtime friendship, Alanna went on, "Like I said before, A.J. never instructs during racing season. You must have an edge those other women didn't. Are you considering racing yourself, perhaps?''

Lissa stared at Alanna in astonishment. "Oh, no! But he's welcome to race all he wants. I'm sure he's as capable a racer as he is an instructor.''

Alanna smiled again. "He makes an even better friend. I should know. I met him when I was a gawky teenager in braces. Don't let that gruff exterior fool you." Alanna winked at A.J. "Maybe you could be more than friends. Nothing would make me and Dad happier than to see A.J. settle down.''

Lissa felt a pleasurable glow spread through her. Not for the first time, she considered herself in the role of A.J.'s latest romantic interest. Once she got her license, he'd be free to see her socially. Although she admired his ethics, she found it frustrating that he was so conscientious about not dating students.

A.J. broke into the conversation. "I think you're jumping the gun a little, Alanna. We're here on business." His voice was unusually brusque. "Lissa, can I get you some more coffee?''

Lissa felt the undercurrents between the two friends and immediately took the hint. "That would be nice, thank you.''

A.J. rose from their table, then said, "Alanna, why don't you give me a hand?''

Alanna looked uneasy at A.J.'s rudeness in leaving Lissa alone, but she did as he asked. Lissa sat by herself, watching the other two walk back to the serving line. They really were old friends, she thought with relief.

But then she frowned at A.J.'s facial expression. Why, they were arguing! Alanna seemed to be disagreeing with something A.J. had said, and her displeasure was obvious.

Well, at least it wasn't a lovers' quarrel, Lissa told herself, fully acknowledging her proprietary attitude. He was only her instructor now, but Lissa was increasingly eager for a different kind of relationship with him. If she passed—no, when she passed—she intended to cross the line A.J. had drawn between them.

Suddenly Lissa's eyes opened wide as Alanna went storming out of the canteen. A grim-faced A.J. returned to the table alone.

"She had to get back to work," he explained curtly. "And we have to go."

"But we just got here! Don't you want more time to visit? What about Wayne?"

"In case you didn't notice, Alanna has cut our visit short."

"It…it wasn't because of me, was it?" Lissa asked, gathering her cup and paper napkin.

"She doesn't approve of something I'm doing," was the cryptic response. "But that's her problem, not mine. Let's go. We'll spend the rest of the day in the air. You'll learn more that way than by sitting here drinking coffee."

Lissa glanced at him, amazed at his sudden bad temper. What had happened?

Three hours later, she was still wondering. A.J. had criticized everything she'd done since takeoff. By the end of the flying session she was exhausted, and thankful to land back at JeffCo.

"Are we flying tomorrow?" Lissa asked as she taxied to the Aerobat's parking space.

"What?" A.J. seemed startled by her question, and Lissa had to repeat it. So much for her ability to hold a man's attention, she thought ruefully.

"I don't know. I'll call you," he said before exiting.

Lissa rushed after him as he headed toward the flight line. "Maybe I have better things to do than wait around for your call," she said boldly.

A.J. stopped his forward progress abruptly. "I beg your pardon?"

Lissa was not going to be intimidated. "You heard me. You've been in a foul temper ever since Alanna left. I may have to put up with your moods when you're teaching me, but I refuse to when you're not." Lissa's chin lifted defiantly. "If you want me tomorrow for lessons, I need to know *now*."

"Oh, I want you all right." A.J.'s face was unreadable, and as she had at the ranger station, Lissa felt vague traces of apprehension.

"What time?" she asked, trying to ignore his disturbing undertones.

"I'll pick you up tomorrow at Hannelly Air Charter right after sunrise. Be ready."

"I will be," Lissa promised.

But for what?

CHAPTER FIVE

LISA WAS STILL ASKING herself that question during the next two weeks. Gone was the fascinating man who had intrigued her. A.J. had once again become the strict instructor. He put Lissa through such vigorous flying sessions that she fell into bed exhausted every night. There were no more pleasant side trips or personal conversations. Instead, she had to suffer through his scathing critiques of her performance. And when she least expected it, A.J. would require her to recover from a stall or a spin or demonstrate some other difficult emergency procedure. Throughout all this, Lissa made two discoveries.

One, she was finally acquiring the very attitude she'd originally scoffed at. Surprisingly enough, once she got beyond her fear and her anger at A.J.'s treatment, she found she was quite equipped to deal with anything he threw her way. The defensive attitude she'd learned became a matter of course, so much so, in fact, that it carried over to her driving. That, too, improved dramatically. Lissa shuddered when she remembered how she'd previously navigated the skies and the roads with her old happy-go-lucky style. She was forced to admit that her previous performance had been far from satisfactory.

The second discovery wasn't as surprising as the first. Lissa realized that A.J.'s company meant more and more to her as time went on. From their very first meeting, Lissa knew he was a man to admire and respect. However demanding he was, however much he drove her to her physical and mental limits, he was always fair. He never asked anything of Lissa that he didn't expect of himself. When Terry once irritably asked Lissa just how much she was willing to take from Andrew James Corbett, Lissa shocked herself by saying, "Almost anything."

That realization shook her even more than her discovery that she used to be a hazardous pilot, and she was unsure how to handle it. A.J. made it clear that he didn't mix business with pleasure. Until she got her license, any romantic overtures from her weren't welcome.

In any event, could she risk getting involved with a man who'd threatened to report Hannelly Air Charter? And if he did report them, then what? Could she still allow him that place in her heart? Lissa didn't know the answer, nor did she know how to deal with her torn loyalties.

No one at home seemed to understand the turmoil she was experiencing. It wasn't often that someone changed noticeably before their very eyes, and Will and Terry were certain that the much mentioned A.J. Corbett had something to do with it.

"If he wasn't teaching you for free, young lady, I would have canceled those lessons long before now," Will announced. He and Lissa had again argued about Hannelly Air Charter's older plane.

"I think his influence over you is quite unhealthy," Terry agreed. "First he tells you that your attitude isn't right for flying and you have to change. Then he tells you this company isn't safe and *we* have to change. If

he told you to jump off a cliff, would you do that?"
Lissa had to turn away from the anger on Terry's face.

Even Leo commented that Lissa was moody and
difficult. "You aren't the same sweet girl you once
were," he concluded.

Only Margaret sided with Lissa, and to all complaints and criticisms regarding her granddaughter,
replied, "Leave Lissa alone. Can't any of you see that
she's finally growing up?"

Lissa had winced at the words, but had to acknowledge their truth. Before, she'd been a sheltered girl
who had allowed the rest of the world to take care of
her. She didn't feel like that girl at all anymore. Now,
more than ever, she felt like a woman. She was an
adult who had to stand up for what she believed, and
convincing Will to give up that dangerous older plane
was her first difficult task. The only problem was that
everyone else still thought of her as the old Lissa. They
assumed she was merely parroting A.J.'s opinions.
Save for Margaret, none of them realized how determined she was, but Lissa refused to back down. She
wanted that plane out of the air, and she wanted them
all to recognize her newfound maturity.

Lissa especially wanted A.J.'s recognition, but he
was still too busy pushing her harder than ever.

"Ready to go?" A.J. asked as they climbed into his
plane once again, shortly after sunrise. He generally
picked her up at home these days.

"I'm always ready," Lissa asserted, mentally gird-
ing herself for the hours ahead, vowing to think of
A.J. as an instructor, not as a man she was attracted
to. "What tricks do you have in store for me today?"

"Not a one."

"Really?"

She was even more surprised when A.J. said, "I'll take the controls. Today you're just a passenger."

"Why?" she immediately asked. "Have I improved that much?"

He just smiled and took over the controls. She noted his flawless takeoff and felt a brief flash of envy. Hers weren't as good as that, but they were pretty darn close!

"I thought I'd let you take a breather today," A.J. said when they were well under way. His voice held a relaxed conversational tone instead of an instructor's firmness. "You've been working hard. You need a break."

"Then why aren't you out on the race course? Why schedule time at all for me today?" she asked.

A.J. shrugged, and Lissa responded with a half-teasing remark. "Don't tell me you prefer my company to racing!"

"Maybe I thought you deserved a reward. You've been doing quite well."

"Quite well?" Lissa echoed. That was the highest compliment she'd received from him. It was music to her ears. "Really? I thought I was progressing, but it's great to hear it from you." She gave him a dazzling smile. "So, where are we going?" She studied the compass, and saw that they were headed southeast.

"I thought you'd like to see some new sights. I, for one, am a bit tired of only flying over Colorado and Kansas."

"I thought you said you had a home here in Golden." Lissa was puzzled. "Do you have relatives or friends in Kansas?"

"Neither," A.J. replied. "Kansas is flat, and I own some property near the border. I've set up a pylon course, and that's where I go to practice. Have you ever been there?"

"No, never."

"Just where *have* you flown?" A.J. asked.

Lissa shook her head. "I've only been on the regularly scheduled flights to the ranger station and to Gunnison for supplies."

A.J. gazed at her in open astonishment. "You've been nowhere else, ever?"

"No. My grandmother and I always wanted to see more of the country, but we're so busy with the ranger station that our planes are always tied up. We never have time for pleasure cruises in them."

A.J.'s face took on that grim expression Lissa had fearfully come to recognize, but it faded as he said, "Then today's excursion will be even more of a treat. Sit back. We're in for a long ride."

Lissa did so with relief. The last thing she wanted was to spoil the pleasant mood with a heated discussion about Hannelly Air Charter's business practices. "What are we going to see? More Indian ruins? I really enjoyed Mesa Verde."

"No, we're not. And no more questions," he said, flashing her a mischievous smile. "I want this to be a surprise."

"Oh. Okay." Lissa felt a warm rush, and it wasn't just from the sun brightly shining through the glass of the cockpit windows. She didn't have to play student today. She could be herself. She took off her light jacket, checked to see that her blouse was neatly tucked inside her slacks and combed her fingers hurriedly through her hair.

"What do you intend to do after you get your license, Lissa?" A.J.'s question came out of the blue.

"Well, I expect I'll fly for Grandfather. I need the experience, and he'll need me, at least until he can get back on his feet financially."

"And then what?"

"I'm not sure."

A.J. gave her a quick glance. "I would have thought you'd join the family business permanently. You know, third generation of Hannelly pilots and all that. You stand to inherit it all, don't you?"

"I suppose. But if I prove that old plane is unsafe, there may not be a business to inherit."

A.J. looked concerned. "You're business is that dependent on the plane?"

"Yes. We can barely keep ahead of our supply runs with two planes, let alone just one. So I've tried hard to discover if the engine's sound. I've gone through all the maintenance paperwork."

"And?"

"On paper the plane seems fine. I've talked to Leo, and he swears he's done his best mechanically."

"That doesn't say much either way."

"I know. I won't be able to find out anything else until I get my license and actually fly the plane myself. That's the only way I'll be able to tell how safe it really is."

A.J.'s voice slashed through the cockpit. "You promised me you wouldn't get into that plane."

"I promised you I wouldn't *ride* in it," Lissa corrected.

"That includes not flying it!"

"What else can I do? For my family's sake, I have to know if it's safe."

"Damn it, Lissa, isn't there anything else in your life besides Hannelly Air Charter?"

Lissa thought about that. "Not really, until..."
Until I met you. She started again. "I never wanted a life in the fast lane. I never wanted to fly in pylon races or become famous or go around the world. I was always content with what I had in my own backyard."

"There's more to life than that," A.J. insisted.

"It's always been enough for me, and I guess it still is—for now..." Lissa glanced down at the vastness of the Rocky Mountains. "They look so beautiful in the summer, almost as pretty as autumn."

"I prefer them in the winter, with the trees bare, the colors gone and their true elemental beauty exposed."

Lissa nodded slowly. Yes, he would, she realized. A.J. stripped life down to its essentials. He never let pretty facades disguise the issues. "I suppose they have a look all their own then," she conceded.

"You don't like the snow?" He turned toward her, his eyes meeting hers. Lissa glanced away, staring blankly through the window.

"I never see a snow-covered peak without wondering if that's the one where my parents are," she said softly. "I suppose you think that's morbid."

"Not morbid, just human."

"They loved each other very much and couldn't bear to be separated. Perhaps their death together was a blessing. Who can say?"

Lissa continued to gaze out her window. "I'm glad it's summer now, not winter." Winter was a painful reminder for people like her—people who were alone.

"Would you grab a stick of gum out of my flight bag?" A.J. asked after a while. "I want to climb a few thousand feet. And while you're in there, grab me that white pilot's cravat, too, please."

"Sure." Lissa unzipped his bag and easily found the two items. She peeled off the gum wrapper, then held the stick out to him. A.J. took it from her with his own fingers and popped it into his mouth.

"What do you want the scarf for?" Lissa asked, feeling vaguely disappointed that his lips hadn't brushed her hand again. So much for wearing her most attractive blouse.

"It's not for me, it's for you. Blindfold yourself with it."

"Blindfold myself?" Lissa frowned at the length of silk. "Why?"

"It's for the surprise," A.J. answered patiently. "Now, be a good student and do what teacher says."

"You aren't going to pull some stunt with the plane and make me recover, are you? I can't very well do that with my eyes blindfolded."

"Don't be so suspicious. I told you, this isn't a regular lesson. I give you my word that this has nothing to do with flying the plane."

Lissa's eyebrows rose in disbelief, but she did as he requested. "How long do I have to wear this? I must look ridiculous."

"Only for a few minutes, and you look just fine."

"Well, all right. But I don't care much for surprises," she said grumpily. "Just fine" was hardly a compliment. Must A.J. be so miserly with his words?

"You'll like this one." She could almost see him grinning at her discomfort. "Total trust in your instructor is required—you should know that by now."

"You said this wasn't a lesson!" Definitely uneasy, Lissa began to rip away the scarf, but A.J. reached for her hand and held it tightly.

"Don't spoil this," he cajoled softly with none of the authoritative edge Lissa was used to hearing. That softness convinced her.

"I won't," she said.

"That's the spirit." Lissa felt his fingertips lightly touch her cheek before he released her hand. This was definitely no lesson. He'd never done that before. "Just a few more minutes, I promise."

Lissa sat back in her seat. "I'm glad my grandfather can't see me now. I just know what he'd say."

"What?"

"I'm crazy." It *was* crazy to give anyone unconditional trust. But A.J. wasn't just anyone.

"Not much longer," he reassured her.

Lissa felt the plane bank and turn. "I wish I could at least see the instruments. Are we almost there?"

"Almost," he said. "Close your eyes while I take the blindfold off. And no peeking."

His fingers drew away the cravat, then gently smoothed the strands of hair that had been mussed.

Lissa shivered with pleasure. "Now?"

"Yes, now. Open your eyes. We're here."

"It's about time. I was getting—" Lissa gasped as her vision was filled with the riot of color beneath her.

A.J. smiled, and appealing little crinkles formed at the corners of his mouth.

Lissa's hands flew to her cheeks in astonishment. Of course, she'd seen pictures of the Grand Canyon, but nothing had prepared her for this. She stared down in wonder, then looked at A.J., totally at a loss for words.

"Kind of takes your breath away, doesn't it?" he said softly.

Lissa nodded reverently, turning back to the spectacular sight of towering buttes, mesas and plateaus in the gorge below.

"No matter how many times I've been here, I never get tired of it." A.J.'s face mirrored her own delight.

"It's...it's so beautiful. And the colors! A.J., I never thought the Grand Canyon had so many! There's every color in the rainbow down there!" Lissa looked down into the mile-deep chasm, amazed by the varied hues.

"Even at its narrowest point, the canyon's four miles wide, so it gets a lot of sunlight at the bottom. Even the best cameras can't do it justice."

Lissa blinked, her hands still on her cheeks. "Look at the rocks! I never saw formations like that!"

"The Colorado River's had a million years to carve those patterns. As long as it keeps flowing, it'll continue to leave its mark."

Lissa's head swiveled from side to side, her eyes drinking in everything. "This is so close to my home, and I've never been here. To think I said I was content in my own backyard. Dear Lord, A.J., I never even realized what was in it!"

She turned toward him again, her eyes brimming with tears at the gift he had given her. Her voice trembled with emotion. "Look what I've been missing all this time!"

A.J. said nothing, but the touch of his hand on hers and the understanding in his eyes was enough. Despite the splendor of the canyon below her, it couldn't compete with the excitement Lissa felt in A.J.'s presence.

Right then she made a silent vow. No matter what, she would never go back to her old way of looking at life. A.J. had shown her that it should be lived to the fullest. She'd missed out on too much already.

"Hey, don't cry!" A.J.'s voice was gruff, and she could tell that his own composure was affected by her reaction. "Look, the canyon's over two hundred miles long. We can't possibly see it all before we run out of fuel, so dry your eyes and make the most of it."

Lissa nodded, rubbing at her eyes with trembling hands. The sights and colors of the canyon below sang to her, and when A.J. wiped away the tears on her cheeks, she felt that if she died at this very moment, she'd never be happier. She rode in silence, impressing these moments on her memory, moments to treasure forever.

Finally A.J. said, "Lissa, I'm sorry, but we have to land. I'm running on fumes."

Lissa gazed at him with a shining expression. "That's okay. I've seen more today than I've seen in my whole life. Thank you for bringing me here."

A.J. nodded. "There's an airport just south of Grand Canyon Village. We'll get fuel and something to eat there."

Lissa feasted her eyes one last time on the majesty of the Grand Canyon. She'd come back, she promised herself. Maybe they'd *both* come back.

Fuel service was quick and prompt. The airport catered mostly to flights for tourists, and the staff were used to pilots to whom time was money.

"You cut it awfully close there, pal," the airport attendant said as he ran the purchase slip and A.J.'s credit card through his machine. "You didn't have much gas left at all."

"I had enough. Besides, the lady wanted to see the sights." A.J. signed the form, then returned the credit card to his wallet.

The attendant took one look at Lissa's face. "First time, I see."

Lissa nodded, her mind still whirling.

"I can always tell," the attendant said. "Now you'll have to come back for the other three seasons. The canyon never looks the same, you know."

"I'll bring her back," A.J. promised, and Lissa felt her heart do a joyous dance. "Come on, Lissa, let's park the plane and go get something to eat."

He helped her down from the plane, giving her shoulders a slight squeeze. "Hey, say something! Or are you going to be speechless for the rest of the day?"

"I just may be," she managed to get out. "In my wildest dreams, I could never have imagined such a thing."

"You must have pretty tame dreams," A.J. teased, but there was no sting in his words.

"Maybe I do. Maybe it's time I changed all that..."

A.J. didn't respond, but after a moment of careful scrutiny, he slid an arm across her shoulders and led her to an attractive restaurant. Lissa could barely touch her lunch, but A.J. did justice to his, then urged her to finish.

"You'll waste away to nothing," he warned.

"Not with my grandmother's cooking, I won't." Lissa stared out the window at the nearby gift-and-souvenir shops.

"Would you like to look inside?" A.J. asked, easily divining her wish.

Lissa glanced at her watch. "I want to buy some postcards or slides of the canyon. Are you planning on flying back tonight? It'll be dark soon, and we may not have time for the shops. I don't want to disrupt your schedule."

A.J. signaled for the check. "Schedules were meant to be broken. I can always get us back later on."

Lissa was pleased that he put her wishes ahead of his schedule. "Then, yes, I'd like to look around, if you don't mind."

So they did. Lissa marveled at how relaxed and easygoing A.J. was as the two of them walked into one gift shop after another. Sometime during their browsing her hand found itself in his.

They wandered through the shops, hands clasped, while Lissa searched for a photograph that did justice to her impressions of the canyon. A.J. finally chose a few slide packets and some postcards for her, since it was growing late. "Ready to get going?" he asked.

Lissa glanced up at A.J. with concern. He looked tired; he'd flown all day, and then they'd strolled through quite a few gift shops. "Maybe we should check into a couple of rooms in the motel we saw," she suggested. "You seem worn out."

"I am a bit tired," he admitted, "but I want to get you home. I wouldn't want your family to worry."

"That's no problem. I can just give them a call."

A.J. gave her a sharp look. "I wouldn't want your grandmother to get the wrong idea. Or your boyfriend."

"Grandma trusts me, and Terry is not my boyfriend."

A.J. lifted one disbelieving eyebrow.

"Besides, how can anyone get the wrong impression from two hotel rooms?" Lissa asked indignantly. "I'll pay for mine, you pay for yours, and we'll head home tomorrow whenever you're ready."

"Sounds good to me," A.J. said after a moment's consideration. "I was up late last night working on one of my racers. But I'll pay for both rooms."

"That's not right. You've done enough for me already. I enjoyed everything about today—especially your company." She gazed up into his face, and suddenly the playful mood changed into something else. There was a tension in the air, a yearning for something more.

"A.J.?" Lissa said hesitantly, her hand still in his. He gently released it.

"We'd better get those rooms now," he said in a firm voice.

Fifteen minutes later, A.J. had them both checked in with an efficiency that Lissa didn't particularly appreciate. It seemed as if they'd been on the verge of discovering something terribly important about themselves. Yet at the first sign of any change in their relationship, A.J. had retreated to his professional persona. Lissa stared into her empty room. He was just across the hall, but he might as well have been across the state. It wouldn't have hurt for him to come in and talk to her for a while, would it? Or perhaps kiss her good-night?

She shed her clothes and stepped into the shower. She hadn't packed for an overnight stay, so she'd just have to rinse out her underthings and sleep naked. Her grandmother wasn't around to be shocked. Neither was A.J., Lissa thought wryly. The idea of A.J.'s being here, now, sparked a tingle of body heat that had nothing to do with the temperature of the shower. Lissa was surprised at its intensity and the sudden direction of her wayward thoughts. Embarrassed, she shut off the faucet and wrapped herself in two big towels.

She'd better call home before she lost *complete* control of her imagination, she decided.

The phone at Hannelly Air Charter was picked up on the second ring. "Hello?"

"Terry? Is that you?" Lissa asked. Usually her grandparents answered the phone this time of night.

"Lissa, where are you? You're usually back by now. I've been worried sick! It's dark outside, you know." Terry scolded her as though she were an errant schoolgirl.

"Please let me talk to my grandmother," Lissa requested, biting back her irritation. She swiped at a drop of water running down one arm and drew the corners of her upper towel closer together.

"They're out. Your grandmother had Will drive her into Gunnison earlier today. And Leo's already in bed."

"Oh. Well, when they get home, tell them I won't be back until late tomorrow. I'm in Arizona."

"Arizona?"

"Yes, at the Grand Canyon. We're going to spend the night at a motel."

"We? Who's *we?*"

"Me and A.J., of course."

There was a sudden coldness in Terry's voice. "And just *what* are you and Corbett doing in Arizona?"

"He wanted me to see the Grand Canyon. Terry, you wouldn't believe it. It's the most breathtaking, fantastic thing I've ever seen in my life!"

"And what does the Grand Canyon have to do with flying lessons?"

"We didn't have a lesson today. A.J. just wanted to show it to me," Lissa explained. "He said—"

Terry cut her off. "When did this professional relationship change into a social one? What comes next? A final exam in the instructor's bed?"

Lissa shot straight up with righteous indignation, her towels slipping at the change in position. She'd just enjoyed the happiest day in her life, and Terry was trying to spoil it.

"It all depends on whether I'm asked, Terry," she coolly retorted, feeling no remorse at hearing his shocked indrawn breath. "Now if you'll excuse me, I have to go. Please give my message to my grandmother. Good night."

Lissa put down the receiver. What *would* she do if A.J. asked?

"So, is he going to ask you, Lissa?" It was A.J., his hand on the knob of the open door behind him.

Lissa's eyes opened in amazement, and she grabbed at both towels. "Please, close the door!"

He did so, but much to Lissa's consternation, he was still inside the room. "What did Terry want?" His face was hard as granite, but Lissa was too surprised to notice.

"What are you doing here?" she demanded.

A.J. stared at her and cleared his throat. "I just came by to bring you this."

He held out a plastic gift-shop bag, but it took him a moment to realize that Lissa's hands were too busy keeping herself covered to take it from him.

"Here." He pulled out a long pink T-shirt with the words "Grand Canyon" emblazoned across the front. "I thought you might want something clean to sleep in. Your door was unlocked. I didn't think you'd be..." He gestured toward her with one hand, the long T-shirt swaying gently over his arm.

"What were you hoping Terry would ask?" His voice sounded oddly unlike its usual self.

"Throw the T-shirt on the bed and turn around," Lissa pleaded. "I can't hold a conversation dressed like this."

A.J. kept staring at her, and finally in desperation Lissa made a successful grab for the T-shirt and a mad dash for the bathroom, where she threw on her jeans and the top.

When she emerged from the bathroom, A.J. still stood where she'd left him, waiting and wary.

"Well?" he demanded. "Are you going to marry him or not?"

CHAPTER SIX

"MARRY HIM? What are you talking about?"

A.J. savagely crumpled the gift-shop bag into a ball, then hurled it at the trash can. "I heard you talking to Terry. You said it all depended on if you were asked."

"You were eavesdropping!" she said with sudden understanding. Lissa sat back down on the bed, relieved. A.J. wasn't mad at her; he was mad at Terry. "And you're jumping to conclusions."

"He didn't propose to you?"

"No."

Some of the stiffness left his face, but he remained skeptical.

"He did a while ago, but I turned him down. Terry's been a friend for years. He's had a hard time accepting that he'll never be anything more. Why, were you worried?" she asked boldly.

"I didn't say that."

"Then what are you saying?"

"I haven't come here to discuss Terry," A.J. said. He nonchalantly sat down in the room's only chair, then reached into his shirt pocket and drew out an envelope. "Here. I was going to give this to you later. You may as well have it now."

Puzzled, Lissa took it from him. She slid a fingernail under the gummed flap. "My license!" Inside was the FAA photo-card, certifying one Lissa Hannelly as a pilot. Lissa read it once, twice and then again, to make sure her eyes weren't playing tricks on her.

A.J. grinned. "Since I was the flight examiner qualified to pass you, it was mailed to me at JeffCo. We'll have to celebrate somewhere special when we get back to civilization. For now, congratulations."

"I can't believe this!" She'd had no idea she'd passed her certification. True, every time she went up in the plane, A.J. had put her through her paces, but he'd never actually said he was testing her.

"When did I pass?" she asked in amazement.

A.J. shrugged. "I'd have to look up the date, but it was soon after you got the plane out of its stall. I put you through the official test soon after."

"Why didn't you tell me?"

"I could have, but I didn't want you to get a case of pre-exam nerves. I knew you were qualified, and I wanted to give you a fair shot at earning your certification."

"So I passed and didn't even know it?"

"Yes." A.J.'s eyes mirrored her own pleasure.

"And this whole trip to the Grand Canyon wasn't a lesson?"

"No. Look at it more as a . . . reward."

Lissa was touched by his gesture. She hadn't thought the day could be any more wonderful—and now this.

"I don't know how to thank you." Her throat tightened with happiness. "Without your help, I couldn't have done it."

"You did all the work. I just helped." He rose to his feet. "I'd better let you get to bed."

Lissa fingered her long T-shirt. "Thank you for the shirt, too."

He shrugged lightly. "It's hardly a designer original, but it was all they had."

"Well, it means a lot, and so does this." Lissa carefully placed her precious license back into the envelope, then laid it on the nightstand. She was filled with pride in her accomplishment, and gratitude toward A.J.

"Please, don't go!" she cried as A.J. started to leave. "I want to talk to you about something."

"I don't think you're dressed for company." His eyes traced the curving outlines under the T-shirt, then returned to her face as he took his seat again.

"But it's important," Lissa said. "It's about my flying."

A.J. made a small grimace of distaste. "I don't want to talk about flying. If the truth be told, I'm just as happy that we're through with lessons."

"You are?"

"Definitely." His eyes took on a sudden gleam. "I told you I don't date my students, remember? Now that you aren't a student anymore—at least, not one of mine—I have a question for you."

"Yes?"

"May I kiss you?"

"I..." Lissa hesitated, but A.J. didn't.

He covered the distance between them in a second and took her into his arms. His kiss was long and tender. Lissa gladly let his lips linger on hers until he reluctantly withdrew to study her face.

"I've waited a long time to do that again," he murmured.

"So have I." Lissa's eyes held the same glow as his, and she reveled in his closeness, his hands on her body.

It wasn't until the cold air of the room hit her bare waist that she reluctantly pulled away. She caught at the T-shirt to stop its upward progress.

"A.J., don't."

"Why? Lissa, the two of us belong together. Can't you see that?" His face suddenly turned hard. "Unless you still think Terry's the man for you."

"Terry has nothing to do with it. I'd just like to know what I'm getting into," she said honestly.

A.J. exhaled with frustration. "I told you when we first met that I was attracted to you. I'd like to know you intimately, and I don't mean just physically, either. I thought you felt the same."

"I do," Lissa said immediately. A.J. called out to her body *and* her soul. "But—"

"But what?"

"I realize I'm not the kind of woman you usually date. I need to know exactly what you're suggesting."

A.J.'s eyes narrowed. "You want specifics?"

Lissa lifted her chin. "Yes."

"We've both admitted we're interested in each other. We both want to spend time together. If it's too soon for us to make love, fine. Tell me. I won't rush you. Is that specific enough, or do you want to hear more?"

Lissa's face fell. "I suppose what I want is some kind of understanding between us..."

There was silence in the room.

"Like a commitment?" A.J. finally asked. "Lissa, I'm not going to offer you an engagement ring. There's no place in my life for marriage and its responsibilities. Is that what you wanted to know?"

"It is." Lissa's voice was a mere whisper. He wanted an affair, nothing more....

A.J. swore, then gently grasped her shoulders. "I don't play the field, Lissa. Nor do I hop from bed to bed. When I'm interested in a woman, it's just the two of us, for as long as we both want it. There would be only you, and only me. No one else."

Lissa could tell that A.J. was serious, and she felt excitement spark through her. She'd wanted to be alone with him from their very first meeting. That was why she treasured her lessons with him so much, despite the hard work and the scares. There were only the two of them in the cockpit, and no one else. Her feelings for A.J.—her love for him—had been growing for a long time. Why should she deny either one of them this opportunity?

Lissa felt sure she could make A.J. want her as much as she wanted him. She had to try. Perhaps if he knew how deeply she cared...

She couldn't back away now. The old Lissa wouldn't have taken this chance. The new Lissa was determined to fight for the man she loved.

"I see." She relaxed in his arms and brought her hands up behind his neck.

"Are you sure about this?" A.J. asked softly. "I don't want you hating yourself—or me—in the morning. Maybe you should sleep on it—alone. Take your time about deciding. I can wait."

"I've decided," Lissa replied, and this time she initiated the kiss. She put all her love into it, all her longing for him, willing him to understand how much she needed him, cherished him.

So it was a shock when A.J. broke away from her. "Lissa, who've you got lined up for your commercial pilot's lessons?"

"You want to talk about *lessons?* At a time like *this?*" Lissa couldn't believe what she was hearing.

"I need to know. Your family owns a charter service. The law says you need a commercial license and a multi-engine permit to fly people and cargo for hire. That's two certifications beyond what you have now. Have you forgotten? And you need to become instrument-rated," he said, referring to the ability to navigate a plane by instrument without the need for landmarks or even daylight. "Especially if you intend to fly in the winter. You know how treacherous the blizzards over the mountains can be."

"I—I haven't made any plans yet," she stuttered. "I didn't even know if I'd get my private pilot's license."

"Damn it, Lissa!" A.J. pushed her none too gently aside. "I *told* you I don't get involved with my students. I should've known you hadn't—"

"I'm tired of being your student! I've graduated," Lissa flung back. "I'm ready for a change! Besides, *you* were the one who started this!"

"True." A.J.'s chin set in a stubborn line. "But that was when I'd foolishly assumed you'd made your own arrangements. Just who else is going to teach you? You know damn well that Hannelly Air Charter can't afford to hire an instructor of my caliber. I refuse to have all my hard work ruined because you've hitched up with some cheap excuse for an instructor!"

"But I wouldn't!" Lissa said, seeing passion replaced by anger in his face. "Let me worry about that. I'll find someone else to teach me, and then we can be together."

"We'll be together all right, but in the cockpit of my plane, not in this bed."

Lissa grabbed at his arm. "But that's what you wanted! That's what I want," she insisted. He was so much a part of her heart and soul already that she craved complete fulfillment. "A.J., please don't leave!"

A.J. shook off her arm. "Lissa, don't you realize? Without a commercial license, you have no future! You're just a dispensable odd-jobs office girl. If Hannelly Air Charter goes under, you'll go under with it. Do you think I'd stand for that?" he demanded.

"I—"

A.J. cut her off. "If you have a commercial license, you can support yourself anytime, anywhere. I want you to have that option, and I intend to see that you get it!"

"And till then, I'm off-limits?" She could barely choke out the words.

"Until you've passed your commercial and instrument ratings, yes."

Lissa thought about all the hours she'd once more be a student, all the days and weeks before A.J. was willing to treat her like a woman. She moaned.

"Stop complaining," he snapped. "You should be thanking me."

Lissa clenched both hands into frustrated fists. "I'm sorry, but I don't feel very grateful just now." Her voice cracked with longing and disappointment, but still A.J. turned away.

He left the room so quickly he didn't even close the door.

THE NEXT MORNING Lissa was wakened by the phone. She groped for it and lifted the receiver to her ear.

"Come on, Lissa, wake up." It was A.J. "We have to leave. It's after seven."

After seven? She'd overslept. Lissa was used to waking around sunrise. She struggled to sit up, the phone still at her ear.

"I'll be waiting for you downstairs in the coffee shop. We've got a long flight ahead of us." Then he hung up.

The morning was bright and clear, and Lissa was able to enjoy one last glimpse of the Grand Canyon before A.J. set the plane on a northeast heading for Golden.

The atmosphere between them was stilted. Lissa struggled to make conversation, although A.J. was unresponsive to her comments about the scenery or the newspaper headlines she'd glanced at in the coffee shop.

"We'll be flying against the wind." She saw from the instruments that the wind was blowing from the north. "Will it take us long to get back?"

"Yes. We'll take advantage of the time to start working on your instrument rating," he said brusquely. "How much trigonometry do you remember from school?"

Lissa sighed, making a determined effort to concentrate. But no matter how hard she tried, a part of her wouldn't be forced away from A.J.

That part seemed to grow bigger and bigger as time passed. Lissa saw A.J. every day as she continued to work toward her advanced certification. He was always the instructor in the cockpit; however, she was delighted to find that attitude softening a little once they were on the ground. She was especially delighted to find that A.J. allowed the time between the end of each lesson and her return home to grow longer and longer. He'd taken to taxiing her to and from her home. They frequently ate lunches and dinners together, but A.J. never forgot her student status. They always stayed in JeffCo's cafeteria for meals.

"What about your racing schedule?" she asked one day. She had obtained her instrument rating, and there were still two more certifications to go. Already it was mid-August; the September races in Reno seemed far too close. "I feel guilty taking up so much of your time. I want you to be prepared."

"I get enough practice in," he assured her. "Why? Afraid I might lose?"

"I worry about your safety," Lissa told him, noting that he seemed more pleased than angered by her admission. "You can't deny that racing is dangerous. Why do you do it?"

"The excitement mostly."

"But since I met you, you don't seem to practice as much as you used to," Lissa observed, hoping for some loverlike admission. She was disappointed.

"Then for my sake, you'll have to get your commercial license and multi-engine rating as quickly as you got your instrument rating."

More than once Lissa cursed the situation she'd created. The delicious anticipation she felt at the prospect of becoming seriously involved with A.J. soon turned into agonizing frustration. A.J. wouldn't even allow the occasional kiss. Although Lissa suspected he was holding himself in tight control, he was always the perfect gentleman.

Lissa didn't know whether to love him or hate him for that. Some nights, as she lay tossing and turning in her bed, she didn't think she could stand the tension much longer.

Her love for A.J. was becoming stronger and stronger. She wasn't just attracted to his looks or his powerful sensuality, although that was certainly part of it. She admired his honesty and clear moral principles. The very fact that he'd taken it upon himself to assure Lissa's future as a commercial pilot, free of charge, was extremely generous. And his insistence on avoiding romantic involvement while they were student and teacher was, if frustrating, certainly laudable.

No matter what A.J. said, though, Lissa knew he'd make a good husband. And if he was as thorough with his children as he was with his students, he'd make an excellent father.

In the next few days she obtained her commercial certification under A.J.'s tutelage. All that remained was getting multi-engine rated. She could hardly wait. At least then she'd have a chance of being a *real* part of A.J.'s life. As things stood now, she was just a student who only saw him inside the cockpit of a plane— or the airport cafeteria. What kind of relationship could she ever hope to build on those terms?

The question weighed on her heart a little more with each passing day. A.J. couldn't help but notice her flagging spirits.

"Lissa, you aren't paying attention!" he said during one lesson. "That's the third time I've asked you to calculate a new heading."

Lissa started, then flushed guiltily. "I'm sorry. I know I should be concentrating."

"That's right, you should." Then in a softer tone he said, "I'll take the controls. What's bothering you?"

Us, she wanted to say. Instead, she shrugged and changed the subject. "The same old problem. I'm still worried about the old plane, and I haven't figured out a way to determine its capabilities without flying it. What with all my lessons, I just haven't had time."

A.J.'s eyes took on a dangerous light. "I told you to stay out of that plane."

"I haven't had a choice," she said bitterly. "Both Hannelly planes are off-limits to me until I mend my ways, as Grandfather says. Grandma sides with me, Terry sides with Grandfather, and Leo plays referee. Every time I see one of them it's confrontation time."

"So leave," A.J. suggested.

"Don't think I haven't thought of it," Lissa sighed. "This isn't a pleasant way to live. But I have to find out about that plane first."

"Why don't you let me fly it? I'm an experienced pilot, and I could handle any problems that come up. At least that way you'll know once and for all."

"This is a family matter, A.J. I want to be the one who decides if the plane is safe or not."

A.J. adjusted the controls. "I don't see how that's possible without someone test-flying it, and you've promised not to. If you won't let me, then let the FAA."

"The FAA?"

"Why not? It would be safer for all concerned. File a report, and have them check out the plane's safety. Not only is it their job, but your grandfather would listen to experts more quickly than he'd listen to you."

"I'm not ready to take that step yet," Lissa replied. "It's easy for you. You aren't involved."

"Aren't I?" A.J. asked quietly.

"You were the one who said there wasn't room for commitment in your life," she reminded him. "So I certainly don't expect my problems to become yours."

"You're wrong, Lissa. They are. Why do you think I've been picking you up from Hannelly Air Charter and dropping you off after each and every lesson? Because I need the practice?"

"I—"

"Or because I care?"

Lissa blinked, unable to hide her sudden surprise. "You don't want me to run the risk of flying in that old plane!"

A.J. flashed her an angry look. "I don't consider you some stranger whose problems aren't my concern, and you know it."

"Maybe I didn't, until just now."

A.J. said nothing, and Lissa realized that her remarks had stung. She hated that, but she was touched by his protectiveness, thrilled by what it revealed of his feelings. Perhaps, she thought as the runway at Hannelly Air Charter became visible in the distance, she could hope for a commitment from him, after all.

"I need to land at the pumps for gas. Let me pay," A.J. said. "I know how tight things are at Hannelly Air Charter."

"I don't care. I'm not taking your money for our fuel. You've never charged me a cent for my lessons, something no one else here sufficiently appreciates...."

"I'm not interested in their opinions."

"It just makes me so mad. Terry always says you should mind your own—"

At Terry's name, A.J. interrupted. "Is he still pressuring you to marry him?"

"No. But this thing with the old plane has really upset him. He believes everything my grandfather tells him."

"Terry's a fool."

"I can handle him. Why don't you call for landing instructions?" she suggested, hoping to get A.J.'s mind off the dangerous subject of Terry.

Unfortunately it was Terry who responded to A.J.'s request for permission to land. He was waiting for her as the plane taxied to the fuel pumps.

"What took you so long?" he yelled before she even had her feet on the ground.

A.J. gave him a cold look, but Lissa tried to calm Terry. She'd rarely seen him this upset.

"I had some problems with my lesson, so we ran over. I'm sorry."

"That's no excuse," Terry complained.

"The lady isn't accountable to you for her time," A.J. threw in.

Lissa sensed trouble brewing. "We need some gas, Terry. A.J. can't get back to JeffCo without it. Would you switch on the pumps?"

"There is no gas. The truck was supposed to be here this morning to fill up our tanks, but we're still waiting. There was a big accident up the Kebler Pass, and traffic is all snarled up."

Lissa sighed. "Great." Kebler Pass was the main route from Denver through the Rockies to Gunnison. "A.J., of course you're welcome to stay until we get some fuel. I'll make up a bed if you want to stay the night, and—"

"Would you stop playing hostess and listen to me for a moment?" Terry broke in.

For the first time, Lissa noticed how agitated Terry was. "What's wrong?"

A.J. drew closer to hear.

"There's been an accident up at the ranger station. One of the rangers—his rapelling equipment broke during a routine climb, and he's badly hurt. He needs to be flown into Denver for medical treatment now!"

Lissa turned to glance at the hangar behind her. Only the older plane was inside. "Where's Grandpa?"

"He's off on a supply run in Gunnison. His supplies are late on account of the traffic backup at the pass. He called earlier and said he wouldn't return until he filled the order. I tried to call him back, but I couldn't reach him. Lissa, we need a pilot!"

"Terry, I don't have my multi-engine rating, and it's after five o'clock now! I can't fly a strange plane in the dark!" She swung around to face A.J., her questioning look immediately answered by his nod.

"A.J. can fly for us," she said with relief.

"Oh, no, he can't," Terry argued. "He isn't insured to fly our planes."

"But he knows how! And his plane's out of gas! Besides, it only has two seats. The injured man couldn't lie down. A.J. *has* to take one of ours."

Terry shook his head, face red with fury. "Lissa, I'm sick and tired of having him try to run our company. I'll go myself before I'll let him take it."

"With your blood pressure? You look like you're ready to explode right now," A.J. said calmly. "Help me get the plane ready, Lissa. We're wasting time. I'll fly it."

"The hell you will!" Terry snarled, and his fist sailed wildly through the air. A.J. neatly ducked, then slammed a punch into Terry's soft midsection. Terry collapsed onto the ground, gasping as he tried to catch his breath.

Lissa looked on in astonishment, her eyes moving from the fallen man to A.J.. "You hit him!"

"He tried to hit me first. Are you going to get me in that plane and off the ground?" A.J. asked in a quiet voice.

"But . . . but we can't just leave him here!"

"I didn't hit him very hard. He'll recover quicker than that ranger who fell down the cliff."

Lissa swallowed. "Of course. Follow me."

She hurried to the hangar, A.J. right beside her. "Do you want me to go with you?" she asked, afraid to get in the plane, but even more afraid to let A.J. risk the flight alone. "You've been flying all day. You must be tired. I can help with the radio and all."

A.J. took one look at the plane and shook his head. "I don't want you in this decrepit thing. Besides, someone will need to tell your grandfather what's going on, and pick Terry up and dust him off."

"Leo and my grandmother must be around, and you said Terry'll be fine. I want to come!" she insisted. The thought of A.J. alone in the old plane was too frightening to contemplate. She would rather be with him than at home, keeping vigil, waiting to see if the plane would stand up to one more flight.

A.J. stopped in his flight check. "Are you worried about me, Lissa?"

"Of course I am! You told me this plane was no good. Now you're about to fly it! Why shouldn't I worry? You made me promise to stay out of it!" Her veins felt like ice.

"I made you promise because you *couldn't* fly this, Lissa—not if it's as bad as I think."

"And you can?" Lissa willed back the tears.

"Yes," he said decisively. "I've got the know-how and experience to cope with a possible problem flight. You don't."

"That might not be enough if something goes wrong!" she cried.

A.J. took her face in his hands. "That, sweetheart, is why you stay here." He kissed her hard on the lips, then set her aside. "Now get out of the way. I have to go."

"You'll radio me as soon as you can?" Lissa begged.

"Will do." He climbed into the plane and gave her a thumbs-up from the window.

Lissa shivered, but she returned the good-luck sign with her own thumb, then ran out of the hangar as A.J. started the plane and taxied toward the runway.

"Be careful," she yelled as the wash from the propellers blew into her face. She watched the plane lift from the runway and begin to climb in the western sky.

Terry had just risen to a sitting position as Lissa returned to the gas pumps. When she tried to help him up, he pushed her away.

"I don't need your help. You've helped enough already."

"You threw the first punch, Terry," Lissa reminded him. "In a court of law, you'd be the one charged with assault. A.J. was just defending himself."

Terry spit out some dirt, then stood up on shaky legs. "It sounds like *you're* defending him. Just whose side are you on, Lissa? Hannelly Air Charter's—or his?"

"I just want the truth about the old plane," she replied. "And A.J.'s helping me to find it."

Terry looked murderous. "Wait until your grandfather hears about all this," he said, staggering toward the house.

Lissa saw her grandmother come outside to meet him and decided to leave Terry to Margaret's more soothing ministrations.

The next hour crawled by. The fuel truck came and went. Lissa busied herself at the pumps, then filled up A.J.'s plane. When her grandfather landed, Terry told Will about the quarrel. His version was vastly distorted, she knew, so she made certain to stay out of Will's way. As it was, her eyes were anxiously on the sky, and her ear was tuned in to the radio out in the hangar. Sooner or later A.J. would have to call in.

The call finally came, and Lissa eagerly grabbed the microphone. Much to her relief, A.J. told her that he'd collected the injured ranger and was on his way, but her relief was short-lived.

"Lissa, I need to land. Is your grandfather back yet?" A.J.'s tone was clipped. "Over."

"He's back, but aren't you going straight into Denver? Over." The wounded man's trip to the hospital shouldn't be delayed by an unnecessary stop here.

"I'm having some mechanical problems, Lissa."

Lissa's heart stopped beating, but before she could say anything, A.J. said, "Make sure your grandfather and his other plane are ready and standing by. Have Leo and Terry waiting to move the patient to the other plane. He's on a stretcher. This is Hannelly Air Charter Two, out."

It seemed to take forever for Lissa to hang up the microphone. "Problems" could mean anything.

Gathering her wits, she quickly ran into the house to tell the men.

Leo, Terry and Will were all ready when the plane finally appeared over the landing strip.

"There doesn't seem to be anything wrong with that plane," Will said, giving Lissa a skeptical look. "It's coming in straight and true. I don't know who's the bigger worrier, you or your instructor."

Lissa ignored her grandfather's complaints. She kept her concentration on the plane, willing it with clenched fists to land in one piece. If anything happened to A.J., she didn't think she could live with herself.

She breathed a final fervent prayer for the safe landing. As the plane drew close, she waited anxiously until she saw A.J.'s silhouette in the dim evening light. She feasted on the sight, staying out of the way until the patient was moved. Will, with Leo along to help, flew to Denver with the wounded man.

Lissa ran out to the runway then, her face alive with welcome, but her happiness faded at his hard-edged look.

"A.J.? What's wrong?" she asked in confusion.

He grabbed her arm and pulled her toward the plane. "Look at this!"

Lissa saw nothing except the evening twilight reflecting faintly from the wing of the plane. "What?"

A.J. released her impatiently. "You can't see it now. It's too dark. But this plane has metal fatigue. You can feel it when you fly, and you can see it if you look. Just how old *is* this craft?"

"I don't know. At least thirty-five years old, maybe more."

"Good Lord!" A.J.'s face was horrified. "That's even older than I suspected. Lissa, your grandfather flies this plane every day. He's too familiar with it to notice the danger, but believe me, I know the metal fatigue's there! The plane shudders and creaks like a rotten staircase. If that ranger wasn't so badly hurt, I would've left the plane at the ranger station and torched it!"

"It can't be *that* bad," Terry scoffed. He'd joined them and overheard A.J.'s words. "Buying new planes whenever you want has spoiled you, Corbett. The rest of us don't mind using older models."

"I'm telling you, that plane is a deathtrap!" A.J. whirled back to Lissa. "I want that plane retired from use, and I want it done *now*."

Lissa thought of her grandfather, and the business he'd struggled so hard to hold on to. "I've tried, A.J., I really have. But he won't ground the plane permanently. He says he can't afford to."

A.J. gave Lissa a long hard look. "If he won't, then I will."

CHAPTER SEVEN

"YOU'LL PUT US out of business! Our contract with the ranger station specifically requires two planes," Terry protested.

"A.J., please don't call the safety board yet. If my grandfather would agree to use only the new plane, couldn't we just leave the old one in the hangar until we get a replacement?" Lissa asked. "That's what we've been doing lately. If we officially retire it, the ranger station would certainly find out. We'd lose our contract for sure."

A.J. shook his head. "That's not good enough. You and I both know your grandfather would continue to use that plane. He'd give *you* the newer plane and fly the old one."

"What do you expect him to do?" Terry's face was red with anger, and Lissa suspected his blood pressure was rising steadily. "We can't afford to buy a new plane right now."

A.J. didn't waver. "If Hannelly Air Charter can't afford proper equipment, then it shouldn't be in business. What would happen if the plane crashed while you were transporting ranger personnel? It's not just your own life you'd be endangering."

Lissa nodded slowly, and Terry made a sound of disgust. A.J. was right, of course. She'd have to try all the harder to convince her grandfather to ground the older craft.

"I'll wait for Will to return, Lissa," A.J. said. "I want to make sure he retires that plane."

"He won't," Terry insisted. "You can wait until doomsday, but Will won't change his mind. I think you should leave—now."

"Then I have no choice. Lissa, I need to use your phone."

"Don't let him, Lissa," Terry hissed.

"Can't you just wait until my grandfather returns?" Lissa pleaded. "I agree with everything you've said, A.J., but it isn't fair that my grandfather isn't here to speak up for the company."

A.J.'s lips compressed into a straight line. "I suppose Will deserves his say. But I'm not going to wait for him to get back. I'll reach him by radio. I've put this off too long already."

A.J. headed inside the hangar, with Lissa and Terry right behind him.

"I'm sure…my grandfather will see reason," Lissa said hesitantly.

"I hope so," A.J. picked up the microphone and contacted Will. Lissa and Terry listened, intent on every word.

"Forget it, Corbett," was Will's immediate reaction. "I'm not making any promises, especially to you. The older plane stays in the air, and that's final."

Lissa took the microphone herself. "Please, Grandpa, be reasonable. A.J. will report us to the safety board if you don't ground the plane."

"Let him!" Despite the static, Will's disdain came through loud and clear. "We'll pass with flying colors. Hannelly Air Charter One, out."

Lissa's fingers clenched tightly around the microphone. She jumped when A.J. gently pried it away from her to hang it up.

"He just threw away our business," Lissa said in a hoarse voice. "He actually believes that everything's fine."

"I was hoping it wouldn't come to this," A.J. said regretfully. He picked up the phone, his fingers poised above the buttons. "Lissa, I'm sorry."

Lissa dropped into a nearby chair. "You gave him every chance," she had to admit. "Even if Grandpa was too blind to take it, you tried." She saw A.J.'s reluctance to call. "Go ahead, phone them."

Terry grabbed for the telephone, but Lissa shook her head. "No, Terry. Let him."

Terry backed down, and A.J. made his call.

"Hello? This is A.J. Corbett. May I speak to Wayne Stevens?"

Lissa lifted her head in confusion. Why was A.J. calling the ranger station and not the FAA safety board?

"He isn't available? Then let me speak to Alanna Stevens, please."

A.J. kept his eyes on Lissa while he waited. He started to say something to her, but then the phone required his attention.

"Alanna? It's A.J. No, I'm not in Denver, and that's why I'm calling. I had to stop and transfer the injured ranger to the other Hannelly aircraft. I want you to give your father a message for me."

Lissa closed her eyes at his next words.

"Tell Wayne there seems to be a problem with one of Hannelly Air Charter's planes. Yes, that's what I said. I'm afraid he'll need to review their crafts to ensure that they meet safety standards."

Terry's curse was vicious, and Lissa flinched.

"The safety of the rangers has to come first. Tell your father to make certain no one gets in that older model. No, I wouldn't even let it land there with supplies. Well, as to *how* bad..."

A.J.'s determination seemed to falter as he looked into Lissa's frantic eyes, then he continued, "It's bad. Very. Look, Alanna, I don't want to get into specifics. I'll let your father and the safety board determine those. Just give him the message, okay? Yeah, I'm sorry, too."

Terry stormed out of the room, the door slamming behind him. Lissa barely noticed, because she was consumed by the suspicion forming in her mind.

"I'll talk to you later, Alanna. No, Lissa has nothing to do with this. She's not at fault. I have to go. Bye." A.J. hung up the phone.

Lights were flashing in Lissa's head. "You told me Alanna's father is an old military friend," she said abruptly.

"Yes, that's right. Wayne was my first instructor in the military."

"When we met, you said you didn't want to teach me because of your racing schedule. And then you changed your mind."

"What's your point, Lissa?" Suddenly A.J. looked wary.

"You said you'd make an exception for me because Hannelly Air Charter had runway access to the ranger station. You implied that you didn't. You said you wanted to see more of Alanna.''

''That's right.''

''No, that's wrong. Alanna said that Wayne always gave you clearance to land. You changed your story, and I never knew exactly why.''

A.J. said nothing.

''So what was your real reason for taking me on as a student?'' Lissa bit down on her lower lip as she thought the unthinkable. ''It wasn't Alanna you were interested in. It was her father....''

''Lissa—''

''That's why you agreed to teach me—so you could spy on Hannelly Air Charter! You wanted to see how our company operated as a favor to your old flying buddy. Didn't you?'' But it was a statement, not a question.

''Drop it,'' A.J. warned.

''I won't! Now I know why you and Alanna fought up at the ranger station. You told her you were sneaking around, checking out our business.'' Lissa felt a tightening in her chest.

A.J. ran his fingers through his hair. ''All right, I admit it. Wayne had voiced his concerns about Hannelly Air Charter long before I knew you. He was worried about the safety of your operation and wanted to cancel your contract, but he didn't have any evidence. When you—an actual member of Hannelly Air Charter—approached me for lessons, it seemed a perfect opportunity to help Wayne out.''

''By spying on us? No wonder you wouldn't let me pay you for my lessons!'' she said. ''What's the matter, did your conscience bother you?''

''Lissa, you have to understand! He's a friend!''

"And you're always loyal to your friends." Lissa lost the battle to keep back her tears. "So what does that make me?"

A.J. moved to reach out to Lissa, but she immediately backed away from him. His hands dropped to his sides and balled into fists.

"Wayne's concerns were legitimate, Lissa. You yourself agreed that the older plane was a hazard. One way or another, that plane has to be retired."

"And pretending to be interested in me—was that part of the plan, too?"

A.J. recoiled as if he'd been struck. "That's not true, Lissa! I care about you—very much."

Lissa took a shuddering breath. "You say you *care*, after all this? You expect me to believe you?"

"Yes, damn it! I care enough not to let you kill yourself in unsafe equipment. I'm glad I turned your grandfather in. Do you hear me? Glad!"

"Are you?" she asked coldly. "I never considered myself a candidate for premature death. But since you did, I'm surprised you even risked becoming involved with me."

"I saw enough needless death in the military. I did what I could to prevent it then, and I intend to do the same now."

"How noble," she said bitterly. "If you knew Wayne was worried, why didn't you just come straight out and tell me?"

"You wouldn't have listened then, any more than you're listening now. You're so worried about hurting your family you're forgetting about all the other people at risk. You can't see the forest for the trees!"

"You didn't trust me!" Lissa felt the tightness in her chest change to stabbing pain. "You didn't even give me a chance! That's what hurts, A.J."

"Lissa, it isn't what you think!"

"It is! But I'm glad I've seen you for what you are." Lissa's voice broke on the last words.

"And what's that?"

"A man with no conscience."

The regret in his eyes disappeared, to be replaced by something cold and hard. His voice was frightening when he spoke again.

"Am I, Lissa? And what do you call the other men in your life? If they'd spoken up seven years ago, your parents might still be alive today."

Lissa's hand flew straight at his face, and the sound of her blow echoed against the metal roof of the hangar.

A.J. rubbed his cheek. He headed toward the door, stopping only to deliver a final parting blow of his own. "When it comes to the real world, Lissa, you still can't see a thing."

Minutes later Lissa heard his plane engine start, and then he was gone. She shivered, whether from shock or the cool night air, she didn't know. It wasn't until her grandmother came looking for her that she finally went back to the house.

Will arrived home later and sent Margaret to Lissa's room to fetch her. Lissa noticed that Terry and Leo had disappeared from the living room, and she wondered lifelessly what Will wanted.

"Terry filled me in on what happened since I've been gone. You have your instrument rating and commercial license, Lissa. Please make arrangements to get your remaining certification from someone other than Mr. Corbett. I don't care what it costs. I've had enough of his interfering. Calling the safety inspectors on us is the last straw. Do you understand?''

"Yes, Grandpa."

That was easy to agree to. The last thing Lissa wanted was the humiliation of seeing A.J. Corbett again. She felt Margaret's hand rest on her shoulder. How much did her grandmother suspect about her feelings for A.J.?

"Once you get certified, you'll help me with the flying as I'd planned."

Lissa wouldn't as easily agree to that. "I won't fly in the older plane, Grandpa. And I won't fly the newer plane at all if I find out you've been transporting anything but supplies in the older one. If you want to kill yourself, that's your problem. But I won't have you taking any passengers with you."

Will stiffened with fury. He started to disagree, but Lissa's resolute gaze was obviously enough to make him reconsider. "I don't like being blackmailed, Lissa."

"Call it whatever you want. Those are my terms." Lissa rose from her seat. She had to escape, get away from everyone, or she'd go crazy.

"Done," Will was forced to agree.

Lissa left.

THE NEXT WEEKS were a veritable hell. After a few days of sleepless depression, Lissa had to face the fact that it was over between her and A.J. Not that there'd actually been much of a relationship, she ruefully admitted. He'd never said he loved her. All he'd said was that he "cared." Well, you could care for a good book, or a pet bird. She'd had enough of his caring.

She decided that their great romance was her one-sided dream more than anything else. A.J.'s failure to call her simply reinforced that conclusion. It was the final humiliation. She started lessons for her multi-engine rating out at JeffCo with a new instructor, her heart dying over and over again each time she saw the familiar Cessna Aerobat—and its owner.

One day A.J. actually came up to her. She felt his presence even before he hesitantly called out, "Lissa?" That alone was strange. Lissa had never known him to be hesitant about anything.

Her heart leapt at the familiar voice, but she forced back her joy. She took a deep breath and greeted him with a chilly nod. "Hello, A.J."

"How are the lessons coming?"

Her eyes flashed with anger and despair. "Is that all you can ask about? My lessons?"

He reached out for her shoulders, but she didn't dare let him touch her. If he did, she'd fall into his arms and lose what little pride she had left.

Lissa took a step backward. A.J. froze, then shoved his hands deep into his pockets.

"I'm sorry I hurt you."

"Are you?" she asked, disbelief heavy in her voice. "Are you sorry you spied on me, too?"

A.J.'s chin lifted defiantly. "No. Since it kept you alive, I'm not sorry at all."

"I should have guessed," she flung out. "For your information, I found a new instructor. I'm doing just fine without you."

Lissa would have left then, but A.J. grabbed her arm and pulled her close. The others in the lounge stared at them curiously, but A.J. ignored them.

"Things go wrong and you immediately put on your rose-colored glasses. That's always been your problem, hasn't it, Lissa? Once, just once, why don't you consider someone else's point of view?"

Lissa felt herself yearning to give in, but she shook herself free. He was the one who'd betrayed her, not the other way around.

"Sorry, but I'm not warped enough to understand yours." She heard his quick indrawn breath; still, she deliberately turned her back on him and walked away.

After that A.J. made no further attempts at contact, although she felt his eyes on her more than once in the airport lounge as she waited for her lessons. She couldn't understand why he didn't go back to the racing circuit, but she didn't bother to find out. Unfortunately the more she tried to put him out of her mind, the more he seemed to occupy it. It was maddening—and heartbreaking.

At Hannelly Air Charter, everyone waited for the safety inspectors to arrive. As with most government procedures, everything took time, and reams of paperwork had to be completed and filed beforehand. Will was hoping Lissa would have her multi-engine rating by the time the safety inspectors arrived. He had Leo and Terry working overtime overhauling the old plane, and both were certain it would pass. Business could then go on as usual.

Lissa wasn't nearly as confident. And if Hannelly Air Charter lost their contract with the ranger station, everyone would be out of a job. She wanted to be prepared to find employment, so she worked even harder on her lessons. If worse came to worst, she'd at least be able to support herself. Her grandparents would be retiring on a very limited budget, and Lissa refused to be a financial burden.

Leo had already made plans to go back east to his family if the older plane didn't pass its safety certification. Terry, however, had no place to go. Lissa was shocked to discover that he still wanted to marry her.

Lissa had been outside, sitting on the wooden bench beneath the trees, trying very hard to review her lessons and not think about A.J., when Terry joined her there.

"I knew you'd come to your senses, Lissa. I'm glad this nonsense between you and Corbett is over. Once we're married, you can find work and support us both until I get a new job. I'm sure I can find something in airport administration."

"Terry, I've told you before, I'm not marrying you."

"Well, not now, but later on," Terry said confidently. "You're much too busy with your lessons to be planning a wedding."

"Terry, please understand. I'm not marrying you *ever*."

"Of course you are." He went on blithely. "We're meant for each other. Once I get my blood pressure down and I have my license back, it'll be smooth sailing. Maybe we can start our own business, like your grandparents."

Lissa turned and her eyes locked with his. "You've been a good friend, Terry, ever since you started working here. I'll never forget how kind you were to me, especially after my parents died. But I'm not in love with you. I'll never be in love with you."

Lissa's words finally seemed to sink in.

"It's that Corbett guy, isn't it? You're still in love with him." The words were bitter.

Lissa couldn't help feeling sorry for him. "I suppose I am. If it makes you feel any better, I'm as miserable as you are." Lissa let her glance drift up to the sky, remembering all the time she'd spent there with A.J.

"I can make you happy if you'll give me a chance." Terry stood up, his serious voice at odds with his teddy-bear face. "Maybe Corbett doesn't want you, but I still do. If you change your mind, I'll be there."

Lissa watched Terry head back toward the house. He seemed determined, but he was no A.J. Corbett, and deep down she knew the difference.

Her multi-engine lessons went on, and Lissa was finally awarded her certification by the new instructor. Now free to fly, she started relieving her grandfather on supply runs to the ranger station, always taking the new plane. Once she found Alanna waiting for her. Not bothering with small talk, the other woman cut straight to the heart of the matter.

"Have you heard from A.J. lately?" Alanna asked as a couple of ranger staff unloaded the supplies from Lissa's plane.

"No," Lissa answered, carefully checking off departing boxes on her clipboard.

"He really cares about you, Lissa," Alanna declared.

"He *cares?*" Lissa echoed disdainfully. "According to whom?" Suddenly the words came tumbling out. "Did he *tell* you he cares about me? That he misses me? Or, heaven forbid, actually loves me? Did you hear him say the words?"

"Well, no, not really, but—"

"I'm not surprised." Lissa made a vicious check-mark on her list. "Because he loves his planes more than he does me. I was just a convenient source of information."

"That's not true," Alanna insisted. "A.J.'s so upset over you he's even quit racing."

"I knew he wasn't racing, but I don't believe I had anything to do with that."

"You're wrong. He hasn't raced since you two broke up."

"We were never a couple," Lissa said bitterly.

"A.J. thought so. He's been miserable ever since—"

"Ever since he used me to spy on our business?" Lissa finished for her. "Since A.J. never bothered to apologize, I find it hard to believe he's suffering sudden pangs of conscience." She started to check off another box on her book sheet and broke the pencil point.

Alanna sighed. "I told him weeks ago to tell you the truth, but he wouldn't listen. He wanted to do it his way."

"I'm not surprised. Rebel Corbett strikes again."

Alanna frowned at the pain in Lissa's voice. "A.J. never meant to hurt you, but you have to understand why he did it. Your company's other plane is unsafe!"

"I agreed with that all along. What I don't agree with are the methods A.J. used to prove his point. He should have been honest with me from the very start." With shaking fingers Lissa reached into her bag for a pen as the two rangers carried more boxes off the plane. "I still would have helped him, but he never gave me the chance. I didn't want anyone's lives endangered, either.''

"Maybe he wasn't sure of that at the time," Alanna said quietly, and Lissa gave her a look of fury.

"Thank you very much. I can see that your opinion of me is no better than A.J.'s.''

"Lissa, I'm sorry! I didn't mean that!''

"Save your sorrys," Lissa said coldly, lifting her chin. "I've had enough of them to last a lifetime. And while you're at it, stop trying to smooth things over for him. If A.J. really *was* upset, he'd make the effort himself.''

Alanna's eyes narrowed angrily. "He tried once at JeffCo, but you turned your back on him.''

Lissa flushed with guilt, then embarrassment.

"Maybe you're right," Alanna said. "Maybe I should mind my own business. It's obvious you don't love him as much as he loves you.''

Lissa watched Alanna stride off, fighting the urge to throw the clipboard at her. How dared Alanna insinuate that Lissa didn't care? Or that A.J.'s unhappiness was all Lissa's fault? He'd brought it on himself! He'd made his choice, and unfortunately Lissa had been caught in the fallout. She hadn't felt this devastated since her parents' death.

Lissa left as soon as the rangers finished unloading the rest of the supplies. As she flew her craft home, she wondered what A.J. was doing right now. Was he as miserable as she was? Probably not, Lissa decided bitterly. He was probably flying some other woman into the sunset and whispering sweet words into her ear.

But no matter how Lissa looked at it, she knew she owed A.J. Corbett one thing. If it wasn't for him, she'd still be that silly girl with the rose-colored glasses. She would never have become a pilot. She would never have been able to stand up to her grandfather. And she certainly would have drifted into a marriage with Terry. She knew without the slightest doubt that he could never make her happy. Lissa refused to speculate on just what particular man could, however.

A few days later at breakfast, her grandfather had an announcement.

"The safety inspectors are scheduled to arrive next week. So far, we're ready for them, but it wouldn't hurt if we all double-check everything."

Everyone nodded obediently, but Lissa didn't see how anything could be improved upon. Her grandfather had gone over the place with a fine-tooth comb, from the paperwork right down to the airplanes themselves.

"Also, we have to finish flying out the last of the fall supplies to the ranger station. In the event our contract is suspended—" Will's face looked as though he believed the chance of that was too remote to seriously consider "—I want our commission for those deliveries. We have at least four planeloads ready to be picked up and flown out of Gunnison, and I want them finished today."

"Grandpa, isn't that an awfully tight schedule?" Lissa asked. "It'll take half a day just to load up one plane, fly it out to the ranger station and unload it."

Will took a hearty bite of sausage, chewed and swallowed, before he said, "We're going to use two planes and make a double run."

Margaret paled. Lissa felt her blood boil at the idea.

"A full load of supplies is just too much stress for that older plane. I won't fly it, and I don't think you should, either."

"You can have the newer plane as usual, Lissa. I'll take the older plane myself."

"Don't, Will," Margaret begged. "Remember Nathan and Rose."

"You worry too much, dear," Will said easily. "You always have. Pass me some more toast, will you?"

Instead, Margaret carefully placed her napkin down on the table and left the room.

"We'll leave right after we finish eating." Will made no comment on Margaret's departure. "Leo, go start up the planes for me, will you?"

Leo lumbered out of the dining room, and only Will, Lissa and Terry remained at the table.

Lissa remembered A.J.'s grim face when he'd returned from flying the older plane to pick up the injured ranger. There was no way he could have faked that fear—and A.J. wasn't a man who frightened easily.

"I'm not flying either plane," Lissa decided. If that was the only way she could keep her grandfather out of the older plane, she would. For the first time, she wished the safety inspectors had been quicker about arriving. She'd never imagined this scenario. So far, she and Will had taken turns flying the newer model.

"You'll fly that plane, young lady, and that's an order."

Lissa rose stiffly, her chair scraping against the kitchen linoleum. "I won't be part of this. I'm staying, you can take the newer plane. I don't want you to disappear like my parents did."

Will's glass slammed onto the table. "I'm the boss here, Lissa. You'll do as I say!"

"No! I won't let you kill yourself. My parents' death was bad enough. I know it was an accident, but what happened should've made you more cautious. I don't want to lose you, too! Grandpa, that plane is just too old for a full load of supplies! Please don't go!"

"I'll do it," Terry broke in. "This company has done a lot for me, and I still know how to fly, whether I have medical certification or not. That is, if you're willing, Will."

"Terry, no!" Lissa cried. Her plan to keep the older plane out of use wouldn't work unless she was the only other pilot. It had never occurred to her that Terry would attempt to fly illegally.

"What are you going to do, Lissa? Inform on me like Corbett informed on us?" Terry mocked. "We need the money from those flights. Maybe you can't see that, but I can."

Will wiped his mouth, then stood up. "At least someone at this table is loyal to the company. Come on, Terry, let's go."

Lissa watched them leave, her hands tightly clenching a chair back. Margaret rejoined her, and Lissa saw that her eyes were red from weeping.

"I'm glad you didn't go, Lissa," Margaret said, her voice heavy with grief. "If only Nathan had stood up to him seven years ago. We all knew the plane was old, but..."

Lissa threw her arms around her grandmother and hugged her hard. "Don't cry, Grandma. Maybe... maybe everything will be all right."

Margaret dabbed at her eyes with a dinner napkin. "It won't be, unless I do something about it. You couldn't stop your grandfather, Lissa, but I can."

"Grandma, it's too late to report Terry. He'll be gone and back long before the authorities can intervene."

"If anything happens to Terry or Will, it'll be my fault. I could have done something before now, but I didn't want to upset you."

Lissa pulled out a chair and helped her grandmother into it. "How can you stop them?" she asked gently.

"If I can prove to your grandfather that your parents died because of mechanical failure, I know he'll stop flying that older plane. Will loved our son, Lissa, but he could never bring himself to face the fact that he might have been to blame. For seven years he's convinced himself that the crash was caused by pilot error."

"Grandma, he may be right. We'll never know," Lissa said. "We don't know where the plane is, so we can't prove it either way."

"Oh, but we can. You see, *I* know where the plane is."

Lissa's mind reeled at her grandmother's statement. "You... you couldn't, Grandma. Everyone looked for it. You remember." Her voice broke as she recalled those painful weeks after the crash. "No one knows where Mom and Dad are."

"I do, Lissa. Your friend, Mr. Corbett, found them for me."

CHAPTER EIGHT

"How?" Lissa's word was a bare whisper. "How could he succeed where everyone else failed?" Here was another secret A.J. had kept from her.

Margaret shook her head. "I don't know, but he did."

"The first time he flew in to pick me up for my lessons, you were so upset... Is that when he told you?"

"Yes. I found out right before you received your private pilot's license."

"But why didn't he tell me? I have a right to know!"

Margaret sighed. "I know, sweetheart, but A.J. said you were having a hard enough time with your lessons. He thought that the news about your parents' plane would just make things harder. So he told me, instead, and left it to my discretion to tell you."

"And I'm supposed to be grateful for being kept in the dark?" Lissa drew a shaky breath. "They were *my* parents, not his!"

"Lissa, he knows that. Mr. Corbett found the plane because you wanted it found. And I'm glad. At last I know where my Nathan is."

Margaret's tears fell onto the table, and she covered her face with both hands. After a few moments, however, she lowered them. "I want to have the crash investigated. I want to find out once and for all what happened. Maybe then I can stop having nightmares about you and Will ending up just like them."

"Grandma..." Lissa watched helplessly as her grandmother hurried from the room. What had A.J. Corbett done to them all?

Mechanically she started clearing up the breakfast dishes. She wanted to go after her grandmother, yet she knew there was no comfort she could offer. To Lissa, the discovery of her parents' missing plane didn't seem quite real. But then, nothing in this crazy mess A.J. had stirred up felt real.

The worst part was that her own emotions were so confused. Yes, she had wanted her parents' plane found, but not under these circumstances. She didn't want her grandmother trying to prove a point with the tragic wreck. And, yes, Lissa knew that the older plane was unsafe, but she'd hoped Will would realize that himself, not be put out of business by a spying stranger.

Worse yet, she'd desperately wanted A.J. in her life, close to her heart. She wanted to be free to love without A.J.'s ironclad principles standing in the way. But no matter how much she tried to fault A.J., she couldn't. His respect for life was too great. A.J. Corbett was willing to give up anything for that.

If only she hadn't been one of the casualties...

Too upset to remain by herself, Lissa decided to seek out her grandmother. Margaret wasn't in the house, so Lissa walked outside and over to the hangar where the office was located. Perhaps Margaret was keeping busy by doing some of the paperwork.

Margaret was there, but she wasn't working. Her face was pale, and her shocked expression revealed every wrinkle, every harsh sign of age.

"Grandma? What's wrong?" Lissa asked, rushing to her side.

Margaret stared vacantly into space. "One of our planes has gone down. I heard it on the radio. I was just coming to tell you."

"Oh, no! Who was flying the older plane, Grandma? I didn't see the takeoff!"

Margaret brought a fisted hand up to her mouth. "I . . . I don't know. I didn't see it, either."

Lissa ran to pour a cupful of water. "Drink this, Grandma. Then put your head down on the desk." The woman looked close to fainting, and Lissa couldn't blame her. Her own knees felt ready to buckle. "That's right. You just rest. I'll get on the phone and see what I can find out, okay?"

The gray head barely nodded. Lissa patted her grandmother's fragile shoulder before reaching for the receiver. "I'll try Gunnison first, okay? Maybe the suppliers heard something."

The suppliers had heard nothing. "They left over an hour ago," she was told. "Everything seemed fine."

Lissa licked her dry lips with a parched tongue. "Can you tell me who was flying the older plane?"

Margaret's head rose at Lissa's question.

"It wasn't Will," the supplier answered.

Lissa mouthed, "It was Terry."

Margaret exhaled in relief for just a second, then her face set in lines of worry again.

"Is anything wrong?" the man asked.

"The older plane seems to be missing," Lissa explained. She quickly cut short the sympathetic murmurs and signed off.

"Exactly where did you hear about Terry's plane, Grandma?" Lissa asked frantically.

"I heard a Civil Air Patrol broadcast with our plane's serial numbers listed. Will must have radioed them in. Terry's such a young man, Lissa, too young to... He shouldn't have flown that plane."

"I'll see if I can raise Grandpa. Maybe he can fill us in." Lissa switched on the radio and depressed the microphone key to hail Will's plane. Despite several attempts, there was no answer.

"He must be out of range," Lissa said, heaving a sigh of disappointment.

"We've got to find Terry!" Margaret wailed.

"I'll call A.J. Maybe he'll let me fly with him. We'll look for him ourselves." Lissa determinedly keyed the microphone again, but as she did, the lights went off inside the hangar office.

"The power's out!" Lissa wanted to scream with frustration. Power outages were a common problem in the mountains. The lines couldn't be run underground, and a good strong wind or a falling tree often disrupted service. Lissa crossed the room to the switch that activated the backup generator.

"It won't work, Lissa. Leo had to order new parts for it."

Lissa put a shaking hand to her forehead. This was like some nightmare she couldn't wake up from. Would it ever end?

"The phones should still work," Margaret reminded her in a quavery voice.

"That's right! Maybe I can reach A.J. that way. I'll call JeffCo."

"Please hurry."

Lissa nodded, but a few minutes later, hung up in dismay.

"What is it?" Margaret asked.

"The switchboard said A.J. flew off earlier. He's airborne. I left a phone message for him. That's all I can do." She forced herself to remain calm. "Let's go back to the house, Grandma. It'll be much lighter, with the windows. We can wait by the phone there."

Margaret nodded and the two of them started walking back. "I think I'll just sit out front," Margaret decided. Lissa knew she wanted to be able to see the approach path to the runway. "Would you make me a cup of tea?"

"Of course. I'll be as quick as I can."

Lissa hurried into the kitchen to boil water on the gas stove, feeling a desperate need to do something. Frenziedly she began washing the breakfast dishes, and as she worked, she tried to think positive thoughts about Terry. But with his medical condition and the poor shape that plane was in, it was easier to imagine the worst. Lissa shivered. Terry had been a good friend to her. And even if he hadn't, she wouldn't wish that kind of death on her worst enemy. If only A.J. would call!

She anxiously picked up the phone to make sure there was a dial tone. The kettle whistled, and she threw a tea bag into a mug and poured. As she put the kettle down, she thought she heard the sound of a plane. She started to run for the door, mug in hand. Some of the liquid splashed onto the floor, but Lissa didn't care. Maybe grandfather was back with good news.

She hurried outside with the hot tea and another small splash burned her thumb. She dumped the contents onto the ground and ran, still carrying the empty cup. When she reached her grandmother, she set the empty mug on the bench beside her. Together they studied the plane on the runway approach.

"That's not Grandpa," Lissa said as they watched the unfamiliar plane taxi to a stop. "Who is it?"

Margaret shook her head in confusion, and Lissa hurried to the plane. Was it the Civil Air Patrol with news? She reached the runway just as its door opened.

A.J. climbed out. His face looked deathly pale; it reminded Lissa of her grandmother's when she'd heard the plane was missing. A.J. didn't even bother to shut off the ignition or close the plane door. He jumped down and ran in the direction of the house. When he saw Lissa, he froze.

"A.J.?" Lissa said hoarsely. That wasn't the Aerobat he usually flew. And he couldn't have received her phone message so soon. "What are you doing here?"

His lips moved soundlessly as he said her name, and then he was sweeping her into his arms and crushing her tightly to his chest.

"Thank God. Thank God. I thought you were on that plane."

"Oh, A.J.," she whispered. Lissa put her own arms around him, trying to still the violent shaking of his body. "I'm all right. I told you I wouldn't get in it, remember?"

A.J. smoothed back her hair with trembling fingers. "I know you did, but when I heard . . . It was on the radio. I was so afraid for you." He hugged her even harder.

"I tried to radio you," he began again, relaxing his powerful grip. "There was no answer."

"That's because our power's out," Lissa gasped. "The lines are down."

"Don't you have a backup generator for the radio?" he asked incredulously.

"It's broken."

A.J. sighed with exasperation. "Of course. I should have known." He sounded his old self again, although he still hadn't let her go.

"I tried to reach you on the phone, but JeffCo said you'd already left," Lissa said. "A.J., the older plane's missing."

He nodded. "I left for here as soon as I heard. How long has your grandfather been overdue?"

Lissa knew A.J. wasn't going to like the answer. "My grandfather isn't missing. Terry took the older plane when I wouldn't."

A.J. uttered a vicious expletive that made Lissa flinch. "Terry doesn't have a license! Don't any of you people have any sense?" he asked furiously.

"You didn't see *me* get in the plane, did you?" Lissa said, tears of worry starting to form. "I couldn't stop either of them. I tried, A.J., really I did. Even if I'd called and reported Terry, I couldn't have stopped him in time. Do you think he's all right?"

A.J.'s anger faded at her distress. "I'm going to go look for the missing plane. I brought my other Cessna. It holds more fuel, and we can search until dark. Are you coming?"

Lissa nodded. "Yes, but let me tell Grandma. I'll be right back."

Margaret hadn't moved from the bench, the empty mug perched precariously at her side. Lissa placed it on the ground. "I'm leaving with A.J., Grandma. We're going to look for Terry. Would you like to come with us?"

Margaret shook her head and closed her eyes.

"Will you be all right?" Lissa had never seen her Grandmother look so old.

"Just go. And be careful."

Lissa gave her a reassuring hug, then ran off to the waiting plane.

The takeoff was sharp, expert and quick. Lissa studied the maps as A.J. climbed. The radio was on, and there was no need to call in for information. The last known coordinates of the missing plane were repeatedly broadcast, as was the area being searched. Lissa marked everything on the map.

"He made it about halfway to the ranger station," she noticed. "And there's hardly any place to land around there, either." Her voice wavered as she spoke.

"You really care about him, don't you?"

"Yes. He's been a good friend to me ever since my parents disappeared. And you know where their plane is," she abruptly remembered.

A.J. said nothing, but he didn't seem surprised at her announcement.

"Why didn't you tell me you were looking for them?"

A.J. frowned. "Why should I? It made no difference whether I was looking or not."

"It made a difference when you found them," Lissa stated.

A.J. exhaled slowly. "So, your grandmother told you."

"Why didn't *you* tell me instead?"

"I'd already stirred things up enough. I didn't want to be accused of using your parents' tragedy to prove my point about Hannelly Air Charter's unsafe equipment."

"That's a terrible thing to say! I would never have thought that!" Lissa burst out, hurt by his low opinion.

"That's news to me," A.J. said harshly. "After being called a spy, a liar and a man with no conscience, I certainly wouldn't be surprised to hear I'd used the dead to achieve my own ends. I have my limits, Lissa."

Lissa felt her face burn with guilt. "I know. And I'm sorry I said those things. But I still want to know where my parents are."

"I'm sure you do, but this isn't the time for it," A.J. reminded her. "Right now, the living deserve our first consideration."

Lissa accepted the binoculars he handed her, taking them out of their case. She silently removed the lens caps, and slipped the strap around her neck. "I hope we find him alive," she prayed.

"So do I. Between the two of us, we'll see what we can do."

A.J. announced his own location, then turned up the radio so they could listen to other reports. He flew a grid pattern, and Lissa painstakingly scanned each area before marking it off on the map. She carefully studied all the places where a plane might be hidden, but saw nothing.

A.J. also scanned the rugged mountains as he flew, but he saw nothing, either. They finally finished their grid search.

"Where else could he be?" Lissa said with desperation. "He's flown back and forth to the ranger station hundreds of times! He wouldn't have flown off course."

"Under normal conditions, no, but if his blood pressure was acting up, he might have become disoriented."

"No, I don't think so. Terry's been doing well with his diet. He was sure he'd pass the flight physical." She flung the map into the back seat. Her nerves were frayed, and her stomach hurt. "His health should be okay. I wish I knew for certain."

"We're doing all we can," A.J. said as he checked the gauges. "We have a couple of hours of fuel left. It'll be dark by then, anyway. It seems no one else has found anything, either." He turned the radio down. "You know, I wonder...did Terry have any favorite spots he liked to fly over?"

"Of course he did, but they weren't anywhere near his normal course for the ranger station."

A.J. considered that. "Terry hasn't been in the air for a long time, Lissa. Maybe he decided to take a scenic route. You know, just for pleasure."

"Maybe he did at that," Lissa slowly responded. "He always liked the Animas Canyon area. That was his favorite air trip. He used to take me there all the time. There are some valleys Terry could land in if he got into trouble."

From the set of his jaw, Lissa could see A.J. didn't appreciate some of that information, but all he said was, "I think we'll swing over that way. Why don't you get on the radio and file a new flight plan?"

Lissa reached for the microphone with rising excitement and did as A.J. requested.

"Would you like a break?" she asked when she was finished. "You've been flying all day."

"Thanks. My eyes could use a rest."

Lissa took the controls, carefully getting the feel of the unfamiliar aircraft. She set the plane on a heading for the Animas Canyon near Durango.

A.J. leaned back in his seat and closed his eyes. After about fifteen minutes Lissa was sure he was asleep, but suddenly he said, "Between you and Terry and your grandfather, I've had more adrenaline rushes with Hannelly Air Charter than I've ever had pylon racing," he groaned. "I hope you don't make a practice of this."

"I don't," Lissa replied. "I only wish I could say the same for the others. Oh, I pray we find him safe and sound."

"So do I," A.J. said, his eyes still closed. "But I'm glad it's him and not you in that plane."

"I promised you I wouldn't fly in it. I always keep my promises," Lissa reminded him, silently thankful that she'd made this particular one. She wondered how much she dared increase her airspeed; if Terry was alive, he might be badly in need of medical help.

After several moments of silence, A.J. remarked, "I heard you got your multi-engine. Congratulations."

Lissa felt a ripple of pleasure pierce her concern. He'd actually kept track of her. "Thanks. I worked hard for it. I had a good instructor, but he wasn't as good as you. I...I've missed you." And then, because she'd admitted that much, she added, "I'm sorry I was so rude to you at JeffCo."

A.J. opened his eyes at that. "So am I. I just wanted to see how you were doing with your lessons. I know for a fact that your instructor was a cranky old codger who couldn't have given you an easy time."

"He didn't."

"Well, it was your choice to find a new instructor, not mine." He sat up and reached for the binoculars.

In these past few weeks, he'd kept even better track of her than she'd realized—which still didn't change the fact that A.J. had used her. Besides, she should be worrying more about Terry than what was over and done with. Or was it?

"Should we map out another grid search?" Lissa asked.

"No." He examined the map, then pointed to a heading. "I think we'll check here first. If I had a plane conk out on me, that's where I'd go."

"Do you want me to spot?"

"No, you fly. I'll spot. Slow your airspeed when we get there, though. I'll have a better chance of seeing anything."

"Will do." Lissa looked down at the harsh granite outlines of the Rocky Mountains and shuddered. If the mountains themselves didn't destroy your plane, the towering evergreens would.

"Look there, Lissa!" A.J. said excitedly.

Lissa did, and blinked. She thought she saw a glimmer on the horizon. A.J.'s finger was already on the focusing knob of the binoculars.

"Well, well, well. Have a look. I'll take the controls now."

Lissa lifted the binoculars from his lap and brought them up to her face. She directed them toward the glimmering object and gasped. She saw a flash of metal, then focused in on the nose of an airplane. The airplane was split in three pieces, and standing next to the wing was Terry, apparently uninjured. He was jumping wildly up and down, waving his arms.

"There's the prodigal son," A.J. observed dryly, "only he won't be coming home for a while yet." He flew directly over the wreck, waggled his wings to acknowledge Terry's presence, then turned around.

"We're leaving?"

"Yes. Terry will have to be choppered out. I'm not risking a landing. We'd never get airborne again. Call in his position, Lissa. Lissa?"

But Lissa, shaking with the strain of the day, sat with her face buried in her hands. Her grandfather was alive; Terry was alive. And that awful plane was destroyed. The investigation into this crash might create problems for Hannelly Air Charter, but never again would she have to worry about the plane causing a loss of life.

As she fought to gain control of herself, she didn't notice A.J.'s silent look of fury at the small figure of the man beneath them. "It's all right, Lissa. I found him for you."

Lissa raised grateful eyes to him. "Thank you. I—I can't ever repay you."

"No, you probably can't," he said abruptly. "Radio in that we've found him. I'm tired. I want to go home."

Lissa did as he requested. Everyone started calling them back, including her jubilant grandfather, and for a while she was kept busy with the heavy radio traffic. There were consultations and congratulations and even a conversation with her grandmother, because the power was on again at Hannelly Air Charter.

Finally A.J. leaned over and shut off the radio. Lissa gave him a look of surprise, but said nothing as she hung up the microphone.

"Are you okay?" she asked him. There was something in his face besides weariness, something more, and it bothered her.

"I'll survive. Would you like to see where your parents are?" he asked suddenly. "We aren't far from there."

Eyes widening, Lissa nodded slowly. She reached for the binoculars, but A.J. placed his hand on hers. Lissa welcomed his touch.

"You won't need the binoculars."

He kept her hand tightly within his grasp as he carefully dropped altitude. They were near the higher peaks of the Rockies, where the snow remained year round.

"This is the same time of day I first noticed anything unusual. The sun was setting, and the shadows were all facing east." A.J. released her hand to point. "They crashed on a western slope."

Lissa trembled.

"I want you to look out your window toward that middle peak directly below us."

Lissa relaxed a little. "A.J., I've been over this area a million times. There's nothing here."

A.J. shook his head. "Look toward that clump of pines that forms the outline of a rough triangle. See it?"

Lissa nodded. It was a group of scraggly trees far above the timberline. They looked harmless enough. "There's nothing out of the ordinary."

"I'm going to drop some more altitude. I want you to look at the westernmost point of the triangle. See that blank area of snow? Look carefully at the outline underneath it."

"A.J., it's just snow and rocks. I don't see—" Her breath caught on a ragged cry. Barely visible under seven years' accumulation of permanent snow and ice was the faint outline of a sheared-off tailpiece.

There was silence in the plane. Lissa couldn't have spoken if she'd wanted to. She could hardly breathe, her throat was so tight with grief.

A.J. took her hand again and gripped it tightly. "It has to be them, Lissa. There were no other planes reported missing in this area."

Lissa continued to gaze down at the faint outline. Usually the area was covered in heavy shadows cast by the shabby, stunted pines and the opposing rock faces. It was only at this particular time of day that the surface of the snow was free of shadows. Otherwise the outline remained invisible. It must have taken A.J. weeks and weeks of searching to locate the remnants of the crash.

"Lissa? Are you okay?" he asked, his voice rough with concern.

"I'm glad I know," she whispered. She turned deliberately away from the tragic outline in the snow and withdrew her hand from his. She meticulously folded the maps, then carefully replaced the binoculars in the case, all under A.J.'s watchful eyes. Tears slipped down one cheek and then the other.

"Lissa, don't..." He touched her wet cheeks with gentle fingers.

"Terry walked away from his crash. Why couldn't they?"

A.J. caught her gaze, and he seemed to take her grief and make it his own. "I can't answer that," he said quietly. "If I could change things for you, I would."

Somehow that made Lissa feel a little better. Seeing that he was as distressed as she was, she gave him a faint smile. "I'm glad I know where they are. This means so much to me. I wish... If there's anything I can ever do for you, A.J., let me know."

"Just be happy, Lissa. Take control of your life. That's all I've ever wanted for you."

Lissa thought about that for a minute. "And what do you want for yourself?"

A.J. said nothing, leaving Lissa to grope for the answer to that question herself.

Lissa's grandparents and Leo were waiting outside in the dark when A.J. landed. Everyone wanted to congratulate him on finding Terry. Margaret hugged both A.J. and Lissa tightly, Leo shook A.J.'s hand, Will was ecstatic. His happiness even spilled over onto A.J.

"I know Lissa filled up your plane, young man, but don't you bother about the cost. Fill up again if you need to. Terry's coming home tomorrow!"

Lissa was disturbed by her grandfather's optimism. Terry had wrecked a plane, a plane he'd been flying without a license. There was no way the insurance company would replace it when they found out. And the FAA would suspend their business charter. But she was too upset about the discovery of her parents' crash site to say anything. Margaret noticed Lissa's confusion and explained.

"Terry passed his health examination last week, Lissa. But he didn't bother waiting for the results, since he's flunked so many other physicals. He had his license back and didn't even know it. The new certification arrived in the mail today after you left."

"Are you sure?" Lissa couldn't believe it.

"That's not all," Will added happily. "I've already talked to the insurance company. Since Terry has his license and the plane's just been serviced by Leo, we're in the clear. We'll be getting a brand-new plane, Lissa! We'll have two planes and three licensed pilots to show the safety inspectors next week!"

Will triumphantly folded his arms across his chest and said to A.J., "Sorry, young man, but we won't be quitting after all."

"I'm sure you'll do very well." A.J. looked straight at Lissa. "Especially you, Lissa. Seeing life through those rose-colored glasses of yours seems to work, after all." His voice was impassive. "Your company isn't even going to be held responsible for flying an unsafe aircraft."

Will brushed aside that accusation with a wave of his hand. "There's no law that says old airplanes can't fly. Even the commercial airlines fly their crafts as long as possible. As long as we keep up with our maintenance and government inspections, we can't be held legally responsible if something goes wrong."

"Grandpa, please!" Lissa wailed. "Just because it's legal doesn't mean it's right. That old plane should have been retired years ago."

"Lissa's right, Mr. Hannelly."

"Don't try to change my mind, young man," Will said.

"I'll leave that to Lissa. Thank you for the fuel."

"A.J., are you leaving already?" Lissa asked, her expression begging him to stay. "We never had a chance to thank you properly for finding Terry."

"You're welcome to sleep over," Margaret added.

"Thanks, but I don't think so. Good night," he said as everyone but Lissa headed for the house.

"What do you mean, I have to make my grandfather change his mind?" Lissa asked as A.J. gassed up his plane. "He'll never change it, A.J., never!"

"You're wrong, Lissa. You're the only one who can make that man see sense."

"Why? Everything's okay now. The old plane is gone."

A.J. turned on the gas pump and swung around to face her with a savageness that alarmed her.

"The old plane may be gone, but the bad pilot still remains. Will thinks he's invincible, Lissa! He needs to be retired as much as that old plane ever did."

"And I have to be the one to do it? Why me? I've done enough already."

"Why?" Lissa had never seen A.J. so angry. "Because you can't go through life carting around excess baggage from the past. Because I don't want to see you dead on account of Will! I don't want to lie awake nights, wondering if you'll make it through the day in one piece. I did enough of that for my friends in the military. I refuse to do it for you."

"You wouldn't have to!"

"Wouldn't I?" he asked. "Could you just walk away from Will and leave your family and their problems behind?"

Lissa closed her eyes. "No. No, I couldn't."

A.J.'s jaw tightened. "Then I suggest you do something about them. I refuse to be your escape valve if you run away. I want a strong woman who comes to me of her own free will. I won't accept anything less." He climbed into his plane.

"Goodbye, Lissa." And then he was gone.

CHAPTER NINE

TERRY ARRIVED BACK at Hannelly Air Charter with only a few bruises. Will gave him a hero's welcome, which infuriated Lissa. She thought Terry should have received just the opposite.

"You flew in a plane that wasn't safe, Terry! And you did it while believing you didn't have a license!" she argued the first chance they were alone.

"But it came in the mail, so everything was legal," Terry said smugly. "Because of that, this company has a new plane."

"That's not the point, Terry! You could have died! Besides, it could easily have been my grandfather crashing instead of you. I was trying to keep him out of that plane, and you deliberately ruined my plans!"

All Terry would do was shrug. "Everything turned out okay, so why are you worried? You know, your grandfather's right. You don't exactly have a lot of company loyalty, do you?" He gave her a strange look, muttering, "I thought I knew you, Lissa, but I guess I don't. Maybe it's a good thing we didn't get married. I have to go. Will's waiting for me."

Lissa was angry that Terry felt no remorse over his little escapade. She was even angrier to find that Will was scheduling Terry for all the flights *she'd* expected to make. Suddenly Terry and Will were the only ones flying—the way it had been before her lessons with

A.J.—and Lissa was being deliberately shut out. But nothing disturbed her as much as knowing the men didn't appreciate her efforts to run a safe business.

The knowledge of her parents' crash site didn't help the situation, either. She didn't tell anyone, not even her grandmother, that A.J. had shown it to her. If an investigation revealed that the plane had crashed due to mechanical failure, it would only upset everyone. For now, Lissa preferred to leave the past alone.

And then came the worst shock of all. While going through the office in search of a file, she discovered that her grandmother had seen a lawyer.

"I can't believe you're filing for a legal separation!" Official papers in hand, Lissa had immediately gone to Margaret.

Margaret took the papers away from Lissa and put them in her purse. "Come on, Lissa. Let's go for a walk."

"But, Grandma!"

"Get a jacket, dear. I'll be waiting for you outside."

Lissa did as she was told, and the two women started out on their familiar path.

"Such a beautiful day, isn't it?" Margaret spoke briskly, her tiny legs easily covering the rocky ground.

"How can you say that?" Lissa felt her depression deepen. A.J. had left her, Terry and Will had deserted her, and now apparently her grandmother was leaving, too.

"When you get older, you'll learn to appreciate beauty, no matter what the circumstances." Her grandmother smiled. "Come and sit down with me." Margaret found a spot on her favorite fallen log and patted a place beside her.

"Are you *really* leaving Grandpa?" Lissa asked with a sick feeling inside.

Margaret picked up a stick and gently twirled it in the air, watching its one remaining leaf dance in the sunlight. "I'm leaving this place, Lissa. If your grandfather wants to come with me, he's welcome. But either way, I intend to go. I'm filing for a separation to show him I'm serious and to make sure I'm taken care of financially."

"You've been married to Grandpa for so long! How can you?" Lissa wailed. Her whole universe was breaking up around her.

Margaret traced patterns in the soil with the stick. "You have to understand, I've spent my entire married life in this one spot. I've been all alone in the middle of nowhere, with only a few people to keep me company. When Nathan was a child and then when you were growing up, I didn't mind. But I'm getting old, and I haven't seen much of the world. My husband owns two planes, yet I've been nowhere."

Margaret shook her head. "I was so jealous when you went to see the Grand Canyon," she said ruefully. "Your grandfather's been too busy with the business to take me there. It's time to go out and see the world on my own. I'd rather Will came with me, but I can't afford to wait any longer. I don't have that many good years left."

"Don't say that," Lissa scolded, but deep down she knew her grandmother was right. "Maybe he'll go with you," she said hopefully.

"With two good planes and Terry to follow him around like a faithful lapdog? I don't think so." Margaret's lip curled in a rare expression of disdain. "I'm so glad you were never serious about Terry. He's a hard worker, but you can do much better for yourself, Lissa.'' She paused. ''Have you heard from Mr. Corbett lately?''

''No. I'm sure he's more interested in racing than in his . . . old students.''

Margaret gave a most unladylike snort. ''Don't be ridiculous, child! Mr. Corbett's waiting to see if you have what it takes to stand on your own two feet. He isn't the type of man to settle for just a pretty face.''

''Grandma, don't *you* be ridiculous,'' Lissa said irritably. She had expected a sympathetic ear in Margaret, not a lecture.

''I know what I'm talking about. You don't want Terry for a husband, do you? Well, Mr. Corbett doesn't want a female version of Terry for a wife.''

''Are you saying I'm weak?''

''At times, yes,'' Margaret bluntly replied. ''Oh, you may show some backbone now and then, but that doesn't mean it'll be there for the long haul. And sitting home and feeling sorry for yourself doesn't go far in proving yourself to Mr. Corbett. But then, maybe his opinion isn't important enough for you to care.''

''It is, too! Don't you dare say that!'' Lissa exploded, then she stopped, her hand over her mouth at what she'd revealed.

Her grandmother's eyes narrowed shrewdly. ''I thought so. Do you love him?''

Lissa thought of all the hours she'd spent with him, of all the times she'd needed someone and he'd been there. She finally admitted what she had never voiced aloud but known for some time. ''I love him more than anything, Grandma,'' she admitted. ''I want to spend the rest of my life with him. But how can I prove it?''

"By stopping your grandfather from flying."

"I—I don't understand."

"Mr. Corbett cares about what's right more than he cares what people think. Maybe he's waiting to see if you feel the same. I don't think he'll settle for a woman who feels anything less."

Lissa nodded slowly. "You know, in a strange sort of way, that makes sense. A.J. always stands up for what he believes in."

"So should you, Lissa. Your grandfather's too old to be running a company. Even with the new plane, his reflexes and his judgment aren't what they used to be. I want you to help me get Will to retire."

"How?"

"I want your parents' crash investigated, and I want you to back me up."

Lissa thought of that lonely white peak in the mountains. "I think they should be allowed to rest in peace."

"No, Lissa. They died because your grandfather refused to face the truth about the safety of his equipment. He let your father use an unsafe older plane, and he made the same mistake with Terry. I love him, but Will's too single-minded when it comes to business. I can't stand by and allow him to make those same mistakes again. I stood by once, and it cost Nathan and Rose their lives. I stood by a second time, and it almost cost Terry his life. I won't do that again."

The pain in Margaret's face showed she had more than paid for her passivity. "Don't be like me, Lissa."

"But Grandpa has two good planes now, and both of them were replacements for crashed ones. Surely he's learned his lesson?"

"No, sweetheart. I know Will. He takes too many risks. He always has."

Lissa thought again of her parents and shivered. "I don't want to know how they died, not after all this time. If we have the crash investigated and find out it was mechanical error, it would destroy Grandpa. Is that what you want, Grandma? Revenge?"

Margaret closed her eyes and tipped her head back, as though to savor the early-autumn sun. "No, Lissa. I want the truth. I've been living a lie for the past seven years by pretending nothing's wrong. And now you're doing it. I don't want to destroy your grandfather. I love him. I want to keep him alive. Why do you think he went on flying that old plane, Lissa?" Margaret asked pointedly.

"He..." Lissa took one look at Margaret's face and couldn't continue. She desperately hoped she was wrong.

Margaret nodded. "He'd rather risk crashing than face the truth. Will loved Nathan, too. I honestly think he'd rather die than admit any blame. And you're just as bad, my dear. You're dying inside, and have been ever since you stopped seeing Mr. Corbett. You'd rather give up his love than face the fact that Will caused your parents' death."

"He didn't!" Lissa exclaimed in horror, rising from the log and backing away. "It was an accident."

"Yes, it was. But it was an accident that could have been avoided, an accident that nearly repeated itself with Terry. You have to help me prove that to your grandfather, for his sake, for my sake and most of all, Lissa, for yours. Because if you don't and you run from this, Mr. Corbett will let you keep on running."

"If A.J. really cared about me, he'd accept me as I am. I shouldn't be forced to abide by his private code of ethics!" Lissa protested, her hands clenched at her sides.

"He's not forcing you to do anything. He's letting you make your own choice. And then he'll make his."

Lissa squeezed her eyes tightly shut, seeing again the faint outline of the tailpiece in the snow. "My parents should be left in peace."

"At what cost to the rest of us?" Margaret asked. She stood up and reached for her granddaughter, but Lissa deliberately stepped back. "Lissa, you're forgetting I loved them, too! Nathan was my only son, and Rose was the daughter I never had. Do you think they'd want you to sacrifice your happiness? My happiness? Will's? And what about Mr. Corbett? He loves you. He's suffering, too."

Tears fell from Lissa's eyes.

"They're dead, Lissa. And what's left of the love in this family is dying, too. But there's still a chance to help us all. Your Mr. Corbett knows that."

"He's not mine, and he knows nothing!" Lissa said violently. "Nothing!"

"You're wrong. He knows you're being caught up in all this, and he's given you a way out. He didn't tell me where your parents are. He only told me that he'd found them. But I'm guessing you know their location—don't you?"

Lissa remembered that lonely expanse of snow-covered granite. "He showed me," she admitted.

"Why do you think he showed you, Lissa, and no one else?"

"Because..." Lissa knew the answer. "Because he wants the decision to reveal their location to be mine."

"Yes. Your decision, and yours alone. He's given you a chance to finally put the past and its terrible influence behind you." Margaret wrapped her arms around herself, looking older and frailer than ever. "It's up to you, Lissa. Whatever you decide, we'll all have to live with it for the rest of our lives." Margaret left, and Lissa was alone in the woods.

She skipped lunch that day. Instead, she filed a flight plan and took the brand-new plane out for the afternoon. She told Will she needed to get the feel of it, but in truth she felt the urge to be alone.

The plane handled like a dream. Lissa's frazzled nerves and troubled spirits were soothed by the steady, predictable rhythms of flight. She flew to all her favorite spots, drinking in their rugged beauty and imposing majesty, finally heading toward the beautiful Animas Canyon. As she did, Lissa found herself reliving her flight to the Grand Canyon with A.J.

She allowed herself to think of him, to acknowledge what he meant to her. He was a man to admire, a man any woman would be proud to love. But what about her? Was she still the happy-go-lucky girl of old, the girl with rose-colored glasses? She hoped not. That wasn't the kind of person she wanted to be, and it wasn't the kind of woman A.J. would every marry. Her grandmother had said he'd demand a woman who was his equal, and Lissa knew instinctively that she was right.

She found her flight path drifting to the west and decided to follow her impulses. She set a deliberate course for her parents' crash site.

The snow still remained on the higher surrounding peaks, as harsh and forbidding as ever. Summer never came here; even the sun, so harsh at this altitude, rarely melted the year-round ice pack. Lissa peered at the ragged triangle of pines and finally pinpointed the crash site. Once again she wondered how long A.J. had searched until he'd found this spot, for all she could see were shadows.

But as she circled above, Lissa felt a sense of certainty that her parents were there. A.J., like Margaret, must hope she'd force her grandfather to retire. And suddenly she knew she had to try. Even though her parents had lain hidden for seven years, the truth about their death had to be revealed. She would have to disturb their lonely resting place.

"I hope you don't mind." Lissa spoke aloud to the shadow-covered snow. "Grandma doesn't think you will. I hope she's right."

She circled the site a few more times, memories of her childhood, of her parents, flooding her consciousness. Reluctantly she faced her plane to the east. She looked down one last time, and pressed a palm flat against the window. "I miss you," she whispered.

Then she headed for home.

SOON AFTER, Lissa decided to call the Federal Aviation Administration and report the coordinates of the crash site. She told her grandmother first, so Margaret wouldn't be shocked when they received the details unearthed by the investigation.

Margaret took the news calmly, then went upstairs to begin packing her bags. "I don't want to be here when your grandfather finds out," she said when Lissa followed her. "I've had enough."

"Do you really have to leave?" Lissa sank down on her grandparents' bed, and Margaret gave her a consoling hug. "Where will you go?"

"I'm going to live with my sister in Florida. We haven't seen each other for years. She's always wanted me to see the ocean, you know."

Lissa watched her grandmother determinedly change out of her work dress into one of her more formal ones, and knew that any argument would be futile. "Do you want me to fly you anywhere?" she asked quietly.

"Thank you, but I've been planning this a long time. I've already asked Leo to take me into Denver. I'll catch a flight to Miami from there. I don't want you to be a part of this. I've left your grandfather a note explaining why I've left and giving him my sister's address and phone number."

"You don't want to stay for a memorial service or anything?"

"No, Lissa. We had a lovely service seven years ago. I said my goodbyes then. But you do what you want about that, dear. I suppose a few more prayers won't hurt." Margaret briskly continued her packing, despite the telltale brightness of her eyes.

"Will you call me?" Lissa couldn't keep the trembling from her voice.

"I don't think so. I'll be very busy catching up on things with my sister. Perhaps we can write to each other later on."

Lissa couldn't believe her ears. It was as if her grandmother was ruthlessly severing all ties.

Margaret must have read her hurt expression. "I need some time to think, Lissa," she explained softly. "I haven't had that for the past seven years. I'll be in Florida until your grandfather comes to get me. If he comes to get me," she added.

She reached for her old jewelry box and handed it to Lissa. "There're a few things of mine I've left, along with everything that was your mother's. I've saved them for you."

Lissa held the box carefully on her lap and watched Margaret put on her coat and matching hat.

"How do I look?" she asked, but Lissa ignored the question.

"Will we ever see each other again?" she asked forlornly.

Margaret hugged Lissa hard, then picked up her two suitcases, waving Lissa away when she would have helped. "I hope so, but if we don't, that doesn't mean we won't still love each other." Margaret was close to tears, but she gave Lissa a sudden, brilliant smile. "If you ever get married, I'll come home for your wedding," she promised.

There was a knock at the door, and they heard Leo's voice. "Are you ready, Margaret? It's time to go."

"Grandma . . ." Lissa whispered.

"Take care of yourself, Lissa. You're on your own now." Margaret studied her granddaughter one final time, then left.

Lissa didn't know how she managed to get through the days after her grandmother's departure. She made her phone call to the FAA, and on the basis of the new evidence, was granted a reopening of her parents' "inactive" case. Investigators were brought in by helicopter to dig through the layers of ice and snow. When their task was finished, her parents' remains were brought back to Gunnison and the verdict pronounced.

The crash was due to mechanical failure, not pilot error.

The story made the local newspapers, as did the announcement of the funeral service and burial. Lissa had to make all the arrangements herself, for her grandfather was a broken man. He had aged before her eyes, first with the news of his wife's departure for Florida, then with the discovery of Nathan's and Rose's bodies, and the FAA's verdict.

Suddenly she and Terry had to carry on the charter business without Will's help. Will sat in the living room hour after hour until the day of the funeral. Even then, Leo had to take him upstairs and help him dress.

Lissa was ready for the funeral early. She and Terry hadn't scheduled any supply runs to the ranger station, so the sound of a plane surprised her. A few minutes later Terry tersely informed her that A.J. Corbett had requested permission to land.

"I'll send him away, Lissa. The last thing we need around here is the likes of him." Terry seemed to be spoiling for a fight, despite the solemnity of the day.

"Let him land, Terry. And try to behave, please," she begged. "He was the one who found my parents. And don't forget, he found you when you crashed."

Terry didn't bother to conceal his anger, although he did as she requested.

Lissa didn't go out to meet A.J., but waited for him to come inside. She didn't think anything could penetrate the feeling of numbness inside her, not even A.J.'s presence. She heard the airplane engine switch off, and then his knocking at the front door.

Lissa didn't have the energy to rise from her chair. Instead, she carefully smoothed the folds of her black dress and quietly said, "Come in."

"Hello, Lissa." A.J. entered, also dressed in dark clothes. He closed the door behind him and looked at her, his gaze one of deep sympathy. "I read about the service in the paper. Is there anything I can do to help?"

Lissa lifted one shoulder in a slight gesture. "Not really. We knew they were d—" She couldn't get the word out, and she started again. "It's been seven years. It isn't as if we didn't know."

A.J. took in the pale face, the red eyes and the weariness that spoke of sleepless nights. "It can't be easy, Lissa. I'd like to be at the funeral, if you don't mind. And I'd like to fly you all to Gunnison. It's too dark to drive, and I don't think any of you is up to the trip under these circumstances."

"Thank you, but Terry's going to fly us. I don't think he or my grandfather would . . . appreciate your company."

"And you, Lissa? Would you like to ride with me?" A.J.'s expression held more than just sympathy.

"How can you ask such a question?" Lissa was roused out of her lethargy by the impropriety of his suggestion. "Someone has to be with my grandfather."

"Surely he has your grandmother?" A.J. wondered, clearly puzzled by her reaction. "Lissa, what's wrong?"

He leaned toward her, and Lissa knew that if she gave the slightest indication, he'd be at her side in an instant. But she made no gesture, no appeal.

Instead she said, "My grandmother's gone."

"Gone?" A.J. couldn't have looked more surprised.

"Yes, gone. She filed for a legal separation and went to live with her sister in Florida."

"She left Will?"

"What did you expect, A.J.? Her son was killed by her husband's negligence, and now the whole world knows it."

"I . . . had no idea she'd react this way. Who would have guessed?" The tightness of the skin over his cheekbones lent credence to his statement. "They seemed so devoted to one another."

"It's my fault," Lissa said wearily, as she stared, unblinking, out the window at the peaks of the Rocky Mountains. "I was the one who reported the crash site. I've ruined my grandmother's life, and my grandfather's, too. He's just a pitiful old man now. He'll never be the same."

A.J. sat down beside her on the couch. He took both her hands and looked straight into her eyes. "Everything that's happened, Lissa, was already a result of their own actions. Your grandfather did nothing to prevent your parents' death, and your grandmother was afraid of doing too much. You can't let it touch *your* life."

"Not let it touch me?" Lissa yanked her hands away. "How can you even say that? Our business is as good as ruined, despite the fact that we have two good planes. Even if we pass the safety inspection, the publicity will prevent us from having our contract renewed. My grandmother has left, and the rest of us have no way to make a living. I've lost Terry's friendship and my grandfather's respect."

She clasped her hands tightly in her lap, determined to prevent their trembling. "And now I have to say goodbye to my parents—again. Tell me, A.J., what was it all for?''

"You did what was right, Lissa. No matter what else, you'll be able to live with yourself."

"That's small consolation, A.J.!" Lissa cried out. "I've lost everything! The price was too high!"

A.J. flinched at the agony in her voice. "Not everything, Lissa. You can still have me." His hands were held out to her, and Lissa knew he was offering her everything he held most precious.

She studied him, weighing everything that had happened since the first time she'd met him. How could she ever spend the rest of her life with someone who'd constantly remind her of the family she'd destroyed?

"I think," she said slowly, "that your price is also too high."

A tremor seemed to pass through A.J.'s body. Lissa rose to stand at the window, her eyes unreadable as she gazed into the distance. When she turned back again, he was gone.

CHAPTER TEN

THE FUNERAL SERVICE, which took place late the next afternoon, was short, as were the prayers said at the burial. The group of mourners was pitifully small, despite the newspaper publicity. Lissa didn't know whether to be grateful for that or not. Somehow it seemed as if her parents deserved more respect.

Will had to be supported by both Leo and Terry during the whole ordeal. With the latter two busy holding Will's limp arms, Lissa was left to herself. She saw A.J. attend both the church and graveside services, and she numbly wondered why he looked so anguished. He'd certainly never known her parents. Maybe he was worried about her grandfather, since anyone could see that Will was dangerously near collapse.

Whatever the reason for A.J.'s distress, Lissa didn't seek him out. Some things had to be weathered alone.

At last it was all over. The final amens were murmured, and the few mourners quickly drifted away. A.J. was the exception. He approached her before she had a chance to get into the funeral car, although Will, Terry and Leo were inside waiting.

"If there's anything I can do for you, Lissa, please let me know."

Lissa felt his hand gently curl around her forearm. "I'll be fine," she said mechanically.

"Will you really?" he asked quietly. "You won't blame yourself for this?"

Lissa didn't answer.

"Or will you blame me instead?"

Lissa was startled out of her numbness. "I did earlier, but I don't anymore. My parents' death wasn't your fault. You aren't responsible for my grandparents' unhappiness, or for mine."

"I never wanted you to be unhappy, Lissa." The blue of A.J.'s eyes fired just for an instant, and he grasped her two hands fiercely. "Will you at least keep in touch?"

With a wave of his hand from the window, Terry signaled her to hurry.

"I have to go," she said, not knowing what to say. "Everyone's waiting."

A.J. dropped her hands reluctantly. He started to turn away, then pulled her into his arms and held her tight. To everyone else, it must have looked like the comforting hug of a fellow mourner, but only Lissa heard him say, "If you ever need anything, just call me. I'll be there."

One hand buried itself in her hair, and he pressed his lips against her cheek. "Take care of yourself, okay?" he whispered hoarsely before letting her go. She felt his eyes follow her all the way to the car. As they drove away, she swiveled in her seat to watch him, a motionless figure in the distance.

Lissa sat in heavyhearted silence during the plane ride home. The funeral was behind her, but there was more unpleasant business remaining. She wasn't looking forward to what she had to do, but she'd left behind the old Lissa for good. She couldn't turn back now.

Once home, Leo and Will went to their rooms. Lissa stayed in the living room.

"Aren't you going to go upstairs and say good-night to your grandfather?" Terry asked.

"Yes. But before I do, I'd like to talk to you."

"About what?"

"Hannelly Air Charter."

"The company?" Terry said eagerly, his face lighting up. "I wanted to discuss our status with you, too, but I thought it was too soon after the funeral. You and I really should make some plans."

Lissa abruptly cut him off. She continued to stand, even though Terry was sitting. "We aren't going to be making any plans, Terry. I'm terminating your employment."

"You're what?" Terry's teddy-bear face took on a tragic air.

"I'm letting you go. I have the authority. I'm in charge of the business now. Grandpa is in no shape to handle things." Lissa calmly smoothed the folds of her dress. She'd had plenty of time to decide about this on the flight back from the funeral.

"But how will you take care of the business without another pilot? You said it yourself—Will's in no shape to handle things."

Lissa stared sightlessly out the living-room window. "That's right. It's time for him to retire, and Hannelly Air Charter with him. In fact, it's long overdue. And I also think it's time for you to move on. Your license has been renewed, and I know Grandpa will give you a good recommendation. You'll be able to find work anywhere."

"I don't want to work anywhere but here!" Terry said with such vehemence that Lissa was momentarily taken aback.

"You don't own this business, Terry, and you never will," she said firmly. "I suggest you start looking for employment immediately. I'm calling the ranger station tomorrow and asking them to find a replacement carrier. Once they do, you're on your own."

"But, Lissa, why?" Terry pleaded.

Lissa took pity on him. "You nearly got yourself killed, Terry," she said gently. "It could have been my grandfather in that plane. You and he are too much alike. You both take too many risks. What happened to my parents is never going to happen again."

Terry rose from his chair. "I can see that Corbett's been at it again." He said the name with distaste. "He's turned you into a hard-bitten cynic, hasn't he?"

"You mean a realist, and I owe him my life for that," Lissa said fervently. "I could have ended up dead. Thank goodness I finally took his teaching to heart. I only wish some of A.J.'s caution would rub off on you."

"It's easy for *him* to be so particular. He doesn't have to earn his living like the rest of us."

Lissa's eyes sparked dangerously. "Even if A.J. didn't have a dime, I know he'd act just the same." She covered the distance between them and held out her hand. "I wish you the best, Terry. I'll never forget you. Even if we haven't always seen eye to eye, you've been a good friend."

Terry refused to take her hand. "And now you're dumping me?"

Lissa sadly dropped her arm. "I wouldn't call it that. But sometimes one has to make choices—the *right* choices. I've realized that. Maybe someday you will, too.''

She left Terry sputtering and went upstairs to Will's room. He was lying down, but wasn't asleep.

''Hello.'' Lissa sat down on the bed and put a gentle hand on his shoulder. ''It's been a rough day, hasn't it?''

Will couldn't look her in the eye. ''You don't have to be kind to me, you know.''

Lissa heard the unspoken question in his voice. ''I still love you, Grandpa.''

Will looked up at that. ''How could you?'' he asked, his old voice rough with grief. ''I killed your father and your mother. No wonder Margaret left me. She must hate me as much as you do.''

''I don't hate you, and Grandma doesn't, either. You honestly didn't think the plane was unsafe. And Dad has to share some of the blame for the crash. He was the pilot. The plane was his responsibility, too. He should have refused to fly.''

Will glanced up, surprised. ''I never thought about that.''

''It's true. Grandma and I just want you to stop taking so many risks. You know she's waiting for you to come and get her.''

''I—I don't believe it.'' Will turned his head away again, his pillow softly rustling.

''But she is. She wants to see the world, Grandpa, and she wants you to take her. Lock up your office, close the business and go! Neither of you is getting any younger.''

''What about everyone else?'' Will asked, his brow etched with worry. ''Everyone depends on me.''

"Terry can find another job. He has his license back. And Leo is as old as you are, Grandpa. He's worked hard all his life. He only stays on because you keep working. If you quit, he'd retire in an instant," Lissa said knowingly.

Will considered that for a moment. "What about you, Lissa?" he finally asked. "Of all people, I owe you the most. I haven't left you much of a legacy, have I?"

"I have my license, thanks to you and A.J. I can find work anywhere." Lissa tried to comfort him. They'd never really been close, but there was a bond between them, even if it was rarely acknowledged. "Let me sell the business for you, Grandpa. Then you and Grandma can do whatever you want."

"Maybe I will." He sat up in bed. "I'll give you the new plane. You can do quite well for yourself with it."

"I couldn't take that!" Lissa said, astonished at his generosity.

"If I retire, I'll only need one plane. You take the other. I couldn't leave in good conscience without knowing you were able to make out. Please, Lissa."

"If it means so much to you—"

Will nodded.

"Then, thank you, I will. You *are* going after Grandma, aren't you?" Lissa asked.

"You've always been an honest girl, Lissa. If she said she'll forgive me, then maybe there's still a chance. I'll give it a try, and if Margaret throws me out on my ear, then it's no more than I deserve."

Lissa hugged him tightly. "She won't."

"I hope not," Will agreed, kissing her on the cheek. He slowly climbed out of bed and reached into the closet for his clothes. "I'd better start packing."

"Why don't you start in the morning?" Lissa suggested. "You need your rest. Today's been an awful strain on all of us."

Will shook his head with something of his old spirit. "I'm not so young that I can afford to waste another day. Your grandmother's a stubborn woman, and it'll take me a long time to get back in her good graces. I'd better get going."

When he'd removed a few items from his closet and laid them on the bed, his strength faltered for a moment. "I'm sorry about...everything. Can you ever forgive me?"

Lissa ran to him and held him in her arms as if she were the grandparent and he the grandchild. "I already have."

Will rubbed a gnarled hand across his eyes, then made a show of busily packing. "I'll sign the plane over to you before I leave. I think Nathan and Rose would be proud of you. I know I am."

"I'm proud of you, too, Grandpa." Lissa knew it hadn't been easy for Will to admit he had been so terribly wrong. "Good night."

Lissa went to her own room. She slowly took off the black dress and started to hang it up, but on sudden impulse wadded it and threw it into the bathroom trash can. She was done with the past. She wanted to look forward to the future. And she would, just as soon as she took care of the present.

Will was as good as his word. The next morning, he flew to Florida. At Lissa's request, the ranger station found a temporary replacement for Hannelly Air Charter. Leo left for St. Louis to live permanently with family. Terry, finally realizing that he'd never have either Lissa or the business, left, too.

"There'll never be anyone else for me," were his parting words, but Lissa suspected it wouldn't be long before he latched on to someone new. Most women fell for his easygoing charm and teddy-bear face.

But not her, not anymore. As Lissa completed the paperwork that would close Hannelly Air Charter for good, it wasn't Terry's face that filled her thoughts.

Lissa sighed. She'd been trying for days to put A.J. out of her mind, with little success. She finished going through the last of the files and gathered up the paperwork her real-estate agent would need to sell what was left of the business. She hoped the agent, an old family friend in Gunnison, was as good as her reputation. She'd miss her home, but if Pamela could sell the place, Lissa would rest easy, knowing that her grandparents had retirement funds.

A week after Will's departure, Lissa dialed her grandmother's number in Florida. Much to her delight, Margaret herself answered, and she had good news. "Will's here, Lissa, and everything's fine. We're both so happy."

Will cut in on the line. "And I'm flying your grandmother to Europe as soon as the sale of Hannelly Air Charter is final. I'm going to show her Rome and Athens and London and—"

Margaret laughed, sounding like a carefree young woman. "Not until we get a buyer, silly. Lissa, where will you live when the place is sold?" she asked, suddenly serious.

"Oh, I'm sure I'll find someplace. I'll look for a job as soon as everything's taken care of here."

"You do that," Margaret replied. "I'll talk to you later, sweetheart. Goodbye."

Lissa hung up, tears in her eyes. They were so happy, and she was so miserable. If only A.J. was here... She remembered his words at the funeral. *Will you keep in touch?*

She would have, if only he'd said, "I love you, Lissa Hannelly."

That would have made all the difference in the world. She could have overlooked anything then, even the fact that he'd used her to spy on the business. But those magic words had never come.

And A.J. hadn't called her or tried to see her since the funeral.

So she kept busy. She packed her grandparents' personal things and sent some to Florida, some to storage. She packed up her own things as she prepared to vacate the premises, and every morning she checked with the real-estate agent.

One morning the agent called her, instead. "We have a buyer, Lissa," Pamela said. "And this party's offered to pay top dollar for your place."

"Top dollar?"

"Yes, you're very lucky. With today's market, I was afraid we'd have to undercut the price substantially. Can you come in this afternoon to finalize the deal?"

Lissa was right on time. "Who's the buyer?" she immediately asked as Pam started handing her legal papers one by one to sign. "Is it someone local?"

"The buyer requested anonymity, Lissa. Do you mind?"

Lissa's pen froze. "Isn't that kind of unusual?"

"Yes, but I checked this person out myself. He's not going to bulldoze the place and build condos or anything," Pam assured her with an apologetic chuckle.

"Still, I want to know," Lissa insisted.

"But I promised! Those were the terms of the deal."

"My grandparents have a right to know who's taking over their home. For all I know, this could be some . . . some criminal!"

"He's not."

"Then why the secrecy? What's his name?"

"My professional ethics forbid it," Pam said primly.

"You can trust me, Pam. Our families are old friends, and the buyer doesn't have to know anything. If you don't tell me, I'm not signing," Lissa threatened.

"Who knows when we could find another buyer, let alone one who'll pay the asking price? You know what the economy's like!"

Lissa stubbornly crossed her arms.

"I can say goodbye to my commission! Come on, Lissa, I have bills to pay, too."

Lissa shook her head.

"Oh, all right." Pam opened her desk and shoved some papers Lissa's way. "There, are you happy? There's his name, and don't you *ever* let on that I blabbed. Now sign this last paper. I'll have your check ready for your grandparents in about twenty minutes if you don't mind waiting. Is that all right? Lissa, are you listening to me?"

She wasn't. Her heart was singing as she read the name of Hannelly Air Charter's prospective new owner. She rose to her feet, purse in hand.

"What about the check?" Pam asked. "Lissa, I need your last signature!"

"I'll sign it later."

"But . . . Are you all right?"

"I'm fine. Just fine."

"Then why leave? What's so important that you can't finalize the sale?"

Lissa's face was all smiles. "Because I think someone just told me he loves me. And I need to know for sure before I sell."

Lissa ran out the door, leaving Pam with a confused expression on her face.

THE NEW PLANE sparkled and gleamed in the noon sun as Lissa set course for A.J.'s other home, near the Kansas border. She'd checked with JeffCo, and they'd confirmed he had no current students. Lissa knew A.J. must be practicing for his next race.

The glint of orange pylons told her she'd reached her destination. She lined up her plane with the runway and landed, then parked next to A.J.'s Aerobat. Before she'd shut off the engines, she saw him striding toward her. He was waiting as she kicked down the stairs of her plane and stepped out onto the concrete.

"This is a bit far from Hannelly Air Charter. Are you out of gas or just lost?" he asked brusquely. To Lissa's delight, though, he couldn't quit hide the joy in his eyes.

Lissa basked in the sight of him, grinning at his attitude—as usual, A.J. wasn't going to make this easy.

"Neither," she replied. "I just thought I'd stop by and say hi, and catch you up on all the latest."

"Such as?"

"Aren't you going to ask me in?"

"Of course." A.J. led her to his home, a large, rambling ranch house as basic and elemental as its owner. A.J. gestured Lissa toward a leather couch in front of a huge picture window and sat down beside her.

"So, tell me your news," he said.

Lissa smiled as she began. "My grandparents are back together. I found a buyer for Hannelly Air Charter, and they intend to go to Europe with the proceeds. They have enough money for their retirement, and then some."

"I'm glad to hear it," A.J. said. Lissa noted he didn't even pretend an interest in the buyer. Instead, he asked, "What about Leo?"

"He retired, too. He's living with his son in St. Louis and loving every minute of it."

A.J. nodded with satisfaction.

"Aren't you going to ask about Terry?" Lissa prompted.

A.J. rolled his eyes upward. "Please say he's moved, at least out of the state."

"No, but the last I heard, he was working at Stapleton Airport in Denver. He's now in airline administration."

"Terry? An executive?" A.J. was incredulous.

"Yes. He's with a major commercial airline. He was always rather good with paperwork, you know."

"No, I didn't. Let's hope he's a better executive than he is a pilot. Thank goodness *he's* out of the skies."

"There's more," Lissa went on cheerfully. "Terry called and invited me to his wedding. He's fallen head over heels for some flight attendant, and they're getting married next month. Shall I have him send you an invitation?"

"I'll pass," was A.J.'s dry response. "And that's enough about Terry. Tell me about you."

"Me?" she said innocently.

"You. You're the only person I'm really interested in. I know a lot has changed for you, what with your parents' funeral and the end of Hannelly Air Charter." His eyes bored into hers. "Why are you here, Lissa?"

Lissa took in a deep breath. "I wanted to thank you. You've taught me so much. I don't just mean showing me how to fly. It's so much more than that. I've learned how to stand on my own two feet. I've learned that I can live with my worst fears. I should have told you this a long time ago."

"And that's all?" A.J. didn't move his eyes from her face, his expression watchful, waiting. Lissa could feel the tension in his muscles as she rested her hand on his arm.

"No, it's not all. I—I know about your wanting to buy Hannelly Air Charter."

A.J. sprang to his feet. "Damn that woman! She promised me absolute secrecy."

"Ordinarily you would have gotten it. But my real-estate agent is an old family friend. I wormed it out of her. I refused to sign unless she told me the truth. I still haven't signed," she announced.

"You haven't?" Anger was replaced by confusion. "But, Lissa, why not? I'm a legitimate buyer. I do want the place, and heaven knows your grandparents have earned their retirement."

"Maybe I'm not sure you *really* want it. I find it hard to believe that a pylon racer wants a second-rate charter business. And I know my grandfather wouldn't want charity."

"It isn't charity!"

"Then sit back down and convince me. I can be as stubborn as you. I'm not signing over Hannelly Air Charter until I know exactly how you feel."

A.J. sank onto the couch, ran a hand through his hair and glared at her, all at the same time. "You want to know how I've been feeling? First, I was afraid you weren't going to report the location of your parents' plane—and then I was afraid you were. Either way, I knew Hannelly Air Charter would be closing down."

"I was so confused when you showed me their crash site," Lissa admitted. "But by then I'd finally faced our company's safety problems. I tried to convince myself that I hated your interfering."

"Only my interfering?" A.J. interrupted. Unspoken were the words "and not *me?*"

Lissa reached for his hand. "Eventually, I realized that I only used you as an excuse so I wouldn't have to face the truth about my parents' death. I was terrified it would be the end of the only family I had left."

"With good reason," he said grimly. "Your fears nearly came true, thanks to me. When your grandmother left and your grandfather wouldn't have anything to do with you, I was really worried. You'd already lost your parents."

Lissa shook her head. "You were right, though, A.J. The safety of the ranger-station staff had to come first. Think how I would have felt if your friends Wayne or Alanna had been killed in one of our planes. Or you!" Lissa shuddered. "I would never have forgiven myself. But no matter how the situation was handled, I probably would have reacted in the same way."

"Why is that, Lissa?"

There was a long silence. Then she whispered, "I didn't want to admit that my parents died needlessly."

A.J. pulled her close and held her tightly. The pain was still there, but the truth, and A.J.'s nearness, made it bearable.

"Their death was such a waste, A.J. My father, my grandparents, even my mother should have realized how unsafe that old plane was. Dad's as much to blame as anyone. A pilot has to take responsibility for his own actions. He should have known better. I firmly believe that now. If it wasn't for you, I never would have faced that fact. I might have died just like them in the plane Terry wrecked."

"You were stronger than everyone, Lissa. I knew that all along, but I was afraid you'd never realize it."

"Is that why you told me where the crash site was, instead of reporting it yourself?"

"Yes. But I wouldn't have stood by a second longer once that old plane left the ground. I miscalculated, though. I never thought Terry would be the one to force everyone's hand. When he took that plane and I thought you were flying it—" A.J. broke off, tiny pinpoints of remembered fear glittering in his eyes.

"But I wasn't," Lissa finished for him. "I'd changed my whole attitude. Isn't that what you wanted?"

"Lissa, changing your flying techniques was one thing. Trying to change another human being is something else—no one has that right. Besides, I didn't want you to change into someone else, since I already knew you were the perfect woman for me."

"You did?" Lissa's face lit up with happiness. This was what she'd waited so long and traveled so far to hear.

"Oh, yes, practically from the start," A.J. assured her. "When I met this stubborn woman who'd flunked her certification exam *four* times but still insisted she wanted to try again, I knew I'd stumbled on someone special. No matter what I threw at you during your instruction, you threw it right back at me, with no tears, no excuses, just hard-nosed determination. I was in love almost before I knew what was happening."

He gave her a tender smile that warmed Lissa to the core.

"By the time we went to the Grand Canyon, I knew you were the woman for me. Those moments we spent together in Arizona meant so much, Lissa. You seemed so happy then. But soon after, everything changed."

He fell silent, and Lissa felt shame wash over her.

"That was when I accused you of spying, and using me. But A.J., you never said you loved me! I didn't know. What made it worse was that I realized *I* was in love with *you*. That's why I overreacted when I found out you only took me on as a favor to Wayne. I thought you didn't care."

A.J.'s gentle caresses spoke of his understanding. "I'm sorry I instructed you under false premises. But if I had it to do over again, I wouldn't change a thing. Lissa, the more I loved you, the more terrified I was of losing you. Closing down Hannelly Air Charter became more than just a favor to a friend. It became personal."

"Because of me?"

"Yes."

"So personal you bought Hannelly Air Charter for yourself?"

"For us," he corrected. "I think we could start a great business. I can instruct, and with Wayne's help and some more pilots, we can get your bid back with the ranger station."

"*If* I decide to sign the papers," Lissa pointed out.

"What are you saying?" A.J. asked, incredulous. "Of course you're going to sell Hannelly Air Charter to me. Will gets his retirement, and you get half interest."

"I don't know if I'm interested in just a business partnership. I still haven't heard you come right out and say you love me."

A.J.'s jaw dropped open. "I have!"

"You haven't! You've put me through torture, A.J.!"

"Of course I love you! Why else would I give up pylon racing? I've even put this place on the market with your unprincipled real-estate friend. What more do you want from me? I'm not one for pretty words, Lissa," he warned.

"I'm not worth it?" Lissa stood up, pretending to be highly indignant.

A.J. grabbed her wrist. "I prefer to show, not tell." A.J. pulled her hard against his chest for a passionate kiss that burned and raged and left her hungering for more.

"Now are you convinced?" he murmured as she relaxed in his arms.

Lissa sighed contentedly. "Show me again. I demand payment for all those lonely nights I spent dreaming of you."

His eyes gleamed with pure male triumph as his lips traveled over hers. "And just what did I do in those dreams?"

Lissa kissed him back, her hands caressing the man she loved. "You did this," she said, "and this . . . and this."

A.J.'s control was soon near breaking point. "Lissa, I think we'd better stop," he said with a groan. He lifted her off his lap and set her on the opposite side of the couch.

"Why? You're marrying me, and as soon as possible if I have anything to say about it," Lissa declared.

A.J.'s face lit up with joy. "I'd already planned on that. We'll call your grandparents and arrange a wedding as soon as they get here. But in the meantime, you'd better stop and let me mind my manners."

"Why should I?" Lissa moved close to him again and put her arms back around his neck. "You never minded your manners before."

A.J. raised a skeptical eyebrow.

"You didn't! You tricked, bullied and scared me into learning to fly. Besides," Lissa replied, nestling even closer, "we've both been sensible long enough."

"Don't you want to wait for the honeymoon?"

"No. I don't want to wait another minute. Let's go to your bedroom."

A.J. pretended to be shocked, but his hands traveled slowly up her sides, his palms warm and welcoming.

"What would your grandmother say? I thought you were a conventional girl."

Lissa edged still closer. "Grandma doesn't have to know. And since when have *you* stopped flouting convention? Aren't you going to live up to your nickname?"

Her voice held so much hope that A.J. broke into laughter. "This from someone who turns the lives of everyone she meets upside down? My love, I'm not the only rebel around here. I can see we're two of a kind."

"Do you mind?" Lissa was confident of his answer, but she wanted to hear it just the same.

"Not at all, sweet Lissa." A.J.'s lips took hers and claimed her as his own. "I wouldn't have it any other way."

HARLEQUIN
Romance®

**HARLEQUIN ROMANCE
IS BETTING ON LOVE!**

And The Bridal Collection's
September title is a sure bet.

**JACK OF HEARTS (#3218)
by Heather Allison**

THE BRIDAL COLLECTION

THE BRIDE played her part.
THE GROOM played for keeps.
THEIR WEDDING was in the cards!

Available in August in
THE BRIDAL COLLECTION:

**THE BEST-MADE PLANS (#3214)
by Leigh Michaels**

Harlequin Romance

Wherever Harlequin
books are sold.

WED-5

WELCOME TO

The quintessential small town, where everyone knows everybody else!

Finally, books that capture the pleasure of tuning in to your favorite TV show!

GREAT READING...GREAT SAVINGS...AND A FABULOUS FREE GIFT!

Each book set in Tyler is a self-contained love story; together, the twelve novels stitch the fabric of the community. The covers honor the old American tradition of quilting; each cover depicts a patch of the large Tyler quilt.

With Tyler you can receive a fabulous gift, ABSOLUTELY FREE, by collecting proofs-of-purchase found in each Tyler book. And use our special Tyler coupons to save on your next TYLER book purchase.

Join your friends at Tyler for the seventh book, ARROWPOINT by Suzanne Ellison, available in September.

Rumors fly about the death at the old lodge! What happens when Renata Meyer finds an ancient Indian sitting cross-legged on her lawn?

If you missed *Whirlwind* (March), *Bright Hopes* (April), *Wisconsin Wedding* (May), *Monkey Wrench* (June), *Blazing Star* (July) or *Sunshine* (August) and would like to order them, send your name, address, zip or postal code, along with a check or money order for $3.99 for each book ordered (please do not send cash), plus 75¢ postage and handling ($1.00 in Canada), payable to Harlequin Reader Service, to:

In the U.S.

3010 Walden Avenue
P.O. Box 1325
Buffalo, NY 14269-1325

In Canada

P.O. Box 609
Fort Erie, Ontario
L2A 5X3

Please specify book title(s) with your order.
Canadian residents add applicable federal and provincial taxes.

TYLER-7

Back by Popular Demand

Janet Dailey
Americana

Janet Dailey takes you on a romantic tour of America through fifty favorite Harlequin Presents novels, each one set in a different state and researched by Janet and her husband, Bill.

A journey of a lifetime. The perfect collectible series!

September titles
#39 RHODE ISLAND
Strange Bedfellow
#40 SOUTH CAROLINA
Low Country Liar

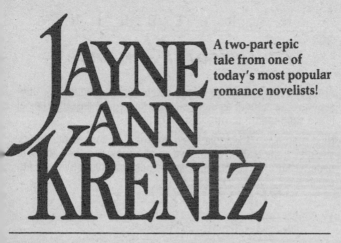

JAYNE ANN KRENTZ

A two-part epic tale from one of today's most popular romance novelists!

Dreams
Parts One & Two

The warrior died at her feet, his blood running out of the cave entrance and mingling with the waterfall. With his last breath he cursed the woman— told her that her spirit would remain chained in the cave forever until a child was created and born there....

So goes the ancient legend of the Chained Lady and the curse that bound her throughout the ages—until destiny brought Diana Prentice and Colby Savager together under the influence of forces beyond their understanding. Suddenly they were both haunted by dreams that linked past and present, while their waking hours were filled with danger. Only when Colby, Diana's modern-day warrior, learned to love, could those dark forces be vanquished. Only then could Diana set the Chained Lady free....

Available in September wherever Harlequin books are sold.

JK92

H A R L E Q U I N
American Romance®

American Romance's year-long celebration continues.... Join your favorite authors as they celebrate love set against the special times each month throughout 1992.

Next month... If Maggie knew college men looked this good, she'd've gone back to school years ago. Now forty and about to become a grandma, can she handle these sexy young men? Find out in:

SEPTEMBER

**SAND MAN
by Tracy Hughes**

Read all the Calendar of Romance titles, coming to you one per month, all year, only in American Romance.